TWO **HEARTS**, TWO **SOULS**, ONE **LIFE**

TWO HEARTS, TWO SOULS, ONE LIFE

WRITTEN BY AUTHOR CHARLES LEE ROBINSON JR.

CHARLES LEE ROBINSON JR.

Copyright © 2025 Charles Lee Robinson Jr. All rights reserved.

No part of this book may be reproduced or transmitted in any form or by any means, graphic, electronic, or mechanical, including photocopying, recording, taping, or by any information storage retrieval without the permission, in writing, of the publisher. For more information, send an email to clrjr.1968@yahoo.com

Casual Comfort Publication, LLC

USA / Florida

My website: amazon.com/author/robinsonc

TWO HEARTS, TWO SOULS, ONE LIFE

In loving memory of my son,

Charles Lee Robinson III

AKA

Mookie

CHARLES LEE ROBINSON JR.

The year 2022 brought my greatest challenge. I lost my only son. I wanted to give up at times, but somehow, I managed to hold it together. They say God won't put anything on you that you can't bear; it must be true because, not with my strength, I am still here creating stories for all of you. So many of my loved ones have died and passed away. The pain is sometimes unbearable. No matter what goes on in my life, it seems that I will always have someone in my corner to keep motivating me and telling me that I am in this world to do wonderful things. I mean, just look at me, I am strong and I can't give up.

I would like to thank all of you who check on me from time to time, those who support me and continue to follow me on social media, and those who buy my books. At this point in my life, you are the reason I continue on my journey.

Again, I would like to thank you from the bottom of my heart.

Thank you,

Charles Lee Robinson Jr.

TWO HEARTS, TWO SOULS, ONE LIFE

There have been many times I've been asked why I write about love, but why not? I believe God is love, and we should inherit that trait from his spirit. I write from my heart and my experiences, bringing realness and authenticity.

Many of us often run from love or hate the word 'love' because of the many bad experiences in our relationships. That's not a reason to give up on love. Regardless, love is all around us, in our families, friends, associates, and beyond.

Love isn't a bad thing; besides, I write about what resonates with my spirit, and it's not necessarily about love - it's about real-life events and circumstances. I craft informative messages and relatable topics for those who want to learn or are eager to share a good word or two about my hard work. As I sit and write, the messages are my own, and I am here to teach. Just remember, we are never too old to learn new things.

This is God's gift to me, and this is God's plan, so I wrote with love and about love until the good Lord doesn't see fit.

CHARLES LEE ROBINSON JR.

TWO **HEARTS,** TWO **SOULS,** ONE **LIFE**

TWO HEARTS, TWO SOULS, ONE LIFE

Written by

Charles Lee Robinson Jr.

CHARLES LEE ROBINSON JR.

FOOD FOR THOUGHT

A woman's place…I am your helpmate…I walk beside, not behind, you… You're my protector…so it isn't hard to find you…God sent me …so I will never leave you astray…I love you dearly…you are my bae…I am your wife, and I will let you lead the way. A woman's place is first place…But I will honor you from day to day…

A man's position…I am your protector…I will carry all the weight… you're my helpmate…and true love is our fate…God put us together…So, I will cherish you along the way…I admire, and I love you…And I am here to stay…I am your husband; I will honor my position from day to day..The love we share…will never be cast away…"I LOVE YOU"

*A **Woman's** Place and A **Man's** Position*

Written by

Charles Lee Robinson Jr.

TWO HEARTS, TWO SOULS, ONE LIFE

TABLE OF CONTENTS

Preface

Chapter 1 – When I first met my wife

Chapter 2 – Past dating issues

Chapter 3 – Our marriage was attacked

Chapter 4 – My confession

Chapter 5 – My relationship was tested

Chapter 6 – Some men don't get it

Chapter 7 – Making sure my wife is pleased

Chapter 8 – Playing spades with the fellas

Chapter 9 – Hanging with the girls at Tasha's house

Chapter 10 – We still have arguments & disagreements

Chapter 11 – Mistakes turn into lessons

Chapter 12 – We can't have children

Chapter 13 – Planning a cruise

Chapter 14 – The Baecation

Chapter 15 – Financial stress

Chapter 16 – Protecting our vows

Chapter 17 – Spiritual growth

Chapter 18 – Playing spades over our house

CHARLES LEE ROBINSON JR.

A **MAN'S** POSITION

SPADE

CHARLES LEE ROBINSON JR.

♥ PREFACE ♥

There's one thing that I love after an exhausting day of work and that's a hot ass shower. It's just something about that hot water on your flesh, yes, I just love it. The thoughts of my day ending on a Friday pleased my heart.

"Brent, Brent Spade, how many times do I have to tell you to take the garbage out, you know they run every Saturday morning," Laquita said. "Honey, I know, I just got out of the shower, can't a man clean his ass?" I said under my breath. I was lucky my wife didn't hear me. "What did you say?" "Nothing, I didn't say anything at all," I said with a smirk on my face. Just as I was getting fully dressed my wife came walking into the room. "Now, what did you say smart, I know you were in here talking shit about me under your breath like you always do." "Like I always do?" "You heard me, you think I don't hear you sometimes, you know I might not be able to see well but I can damn sure hear." "Ha, ha, but you do have those Mr. Spok ears." "Shut up talking about my ears and hurry up and take the garbage out." "Didn't you say they are coming in the morning?" "Brent Spade, go." She said as she pointed her finger towards the door. I didn't say anything else; I just did what my beautiful wife wanted.

Most men often feel it's a sign of weakness for a man to listen to his wife, but not me. I love my wife, and I know that for our marriage to work, I must be willing to listen to her and please her, and vice versa. She listens and pleases me too; you'll see.

After I returned to the house from taking the garbage out, I washed my hands at the kitchen sink and sat on the sofa. Laquita walked in with a smile on her face.

"Thank you, Bae, for taking out the garbage." She said as she kissed my lips softly. "Okay now, you better stop that, before you make Mr. Willie grow." "Oh yeah, Mr. Spade, are you threatening me with a good time?" She grabbed my package with a firm grip. "Okay, now, I am warning you." "Ha, ha, ooh, he's growing too, I better stop, I have things to do this morning," "Oh yeah, like what?" "First, I have to take a shower and then meet the girls out." "Baby, the girls can wait, now you got me horny, I want some." "Calm that long tally wacker down, at least until later." "So, your girls are more important than me and Mr. Willie?" "Don't start, you know that's a lie, because Mr. Willie is good, good, daddy, but I did promise the girls and now I am running late, I promise to let you have all of me tonight." "You promise?" Yes, now let me get out of here." "Hold up a second, since you're out, can you take my clothes to the cleaners?" "Uhm, yeah, where are they?" "I laid them on the washer and dryer in the laundry room." "You mean those sports jackets and those white jeans." "Yes, that's it." "Honey, you're late, I already took those two days ago to the cleaners." "You did, damn, you're good, come here and let me get another one of those juicy ass kisses, bring those juicy lips over here." "You mean these?" "Yes," I said as I kissed her and then put her hand on Mr. Willie. "Ooh, you're so nasty, you better stop, now damn you're making my kitty hot, man, let me go, I have to go." She said as she slowly pulled away and at the same time slowly caressed Mr. Willie as she pulled back.

"I love you, Mr. Spade, and you too, Mr. Willie, ha, ha." She said as she giggled. "I love you, too, Mrs. Spade. I suppose I'll hang out with the guys for a while. Call me when you're done." "I will, oh, I have to go, I'm late, late, messing with you, I love you." She said as she kissed me quickly and ran upstairs to shower.

I couldn't do anything but smile. I love my wife and I am glad we gel the way we do, but I must admit, it has been a long journey.

1

WHEN I FIRST MET MY WIFE

IN THE PAST:

"Hey, Brent, look down the street, a new family is moving into old man Darrel's house." "Old man Darrel's house, do they know he died in that house?" "I guess they don't, and look, they have a daughter." "A daughter, how do you know?" "Duh, dummy, I just rode my bike there and waved." "You waved, and what did they do?" "The parents waved, but she put her head down." "That's because she doesn't like you, you're ugly." "Man, you are ugly too. She didn't wave because she didn't know me. I'm not ugly, am I?" "Ha, ha, of course, you are, but you're still my best friend, Steven." "Man, you're wrong, I bet you, she won't wave at you either, now ride down and see." "How much do you want to bet she waves at me?" "I don't have any money, but I will

bet you a chico stick and some now and later," Steven said. "Okay, bet," I said as I jumped on my bike, and I rode down by the new neighbors.

The young girl was standing on the porch while her parents were taking things into the house. I rode by slowly and I said, "Hi, I'm Brent, are y'all moving in?" "Hi, yes we are, oh, and I'm Laquita." She said as she waved at me. I immediately looked down at the street where Steven was looking, and I nodded my head.

"That was it, he lost the bet, and Laquita and I have been talking ever since, although there were some breakups along the way."

"So, you got her to wave just like that, huh?" My friend Carlos asked. "Just like that, isn't that right, Steven?" I asked. "I don't know what you're talking about," Steven said with a chuckle. "He does not want to admit it, but that chico stick was good, good," I said as I started laughing. "Whatever, man, that was centuries ago," Steven said. "So, how long have you known Laquita, again?" My friend Stanley asked. "It's been well over twenty-five years, we've been married for, I think, seventeen years," I said. "Damn, that's a long ass time," Carlos said. "His ass is pussy whipped," Steven said. "You're just jealous," I said. "Jealous, jealous of what, if it weren't for me, you guys would have never met one another," Steven said. "Oh, now you're trying to take all the credit?" Stanley said with a smirk on his face. "Exactly," I said. "Man, get out of here, you're just mad because she didn't wave at you because you're ugly," Carlos said. "Ha, ha, I told him," I added. "Man, shut up, I am not jealous and I am not ugly, my momma said I was handsome," Steven said. "Then your momma lied," Carlos said, and we all started laughing. "Man, I want to know how you guys keep your marriage going, because hell, I can't keep a woman past two months," Stanley said. "That's because you're lame and you don't have any game," Steven said. "Man, shut up, aren't you single?" Carlos asked. "Yes, I am happily single," Steven said, and we laughed. "You're stupid, boy, who says they're happily single?" Stanley asked. "Me, that's who, next question," Steven said.

"This crazy fool here, now to answer your question, Carlos, it takes time, patience, and respect, and oh yeah, don't forget honesty," I said. "I think I am an honest guy," Carlos said. "If you have to think about being an honest guy, then that's the problem," I said. "This fool is lame too, just like him," Steven said as he tilted his head towards Stanley. "Fuck you," Carlos said as he stuck his middle finger at Steven. "So, y'all have been together for all this time without problems?" Stanley asked. "Hell, yeah, every relationship has problems, it just takes a lot of communication, and trying to walk in each other's shoes," I said. "Each other's shoes, what the hell does that mean?" Stanley asked with curiosity. "You have to try to walk in the other person's shoes, try to understand where they're coming from, you know, try to be empathetic," I said. "Okay, I get it, I think," Stanley said. "Man, you don't get shit, you're just like Mr. Lame over here,"

TWO HEARTS, TWO SOULS, ONE LIFE

Steven said to Stanley. "Who's talking to you anyway, ugly boy, you probably haven't had any pussy, since it had you," Stanley said to Steven, and we all started laughing. "Hey, hey, this is my best friend ya'll scoring on," I said in laughter. "Hell, if I were you, I wouldn't tell nobody that shit," Carlos said in laughter. "That's right, when the last time you had a woman anyway, exactly, when they were handing out welfare cheese and that was over twenty years ago, and oh yeah, old girl, stank Tangee, don't count because she was blind, ha, ha," Stanley said and we laughed until we cried.

"Well, listen, guys, I have to go, I will tell y'all some of the stories about me and Laquita the next time we get together," I said. "All right, Brent, hey, I am going to call you later, I may need some advice," Carlos said. "Yeah, me too," Stanley said. "Both of ya'll are helpless, ya'll cannot keep a woman if your lives depended on it," Steven said. "Ugly homeless boy, go back and sleep under that bridge downtown, ha, ha," Stanley said to Steven. "Ya'll bad, boy, I have to go," I said. "Yeah, get home, before your boss, your wife put her foot in your ass for not taking out the garbage again," Steven said. "Fuck you, you're just a hater," I said as I stuck up my middle finger. "Man, that's not nice, you know I love you, bro, I was only playing," Steven said as I walked away. "You rubbed Brent the wrong way." I heard Carlos say. "Damn, he threw the F-bomb at you," Stanley said. "He'll be okay. Do you guys really think I am ugly?" Steven asked. "Yeah, butt ugly," Stanley said and we all started laughing as I drove off in my BMW with the windows lowered. I arrived home around the same time as Laquita. "Hey, honey, how was your outing with the fellas?" "It was okay, it was nice to see those fools." "You guys had fun, huh?" "We did, what about you and the ladies, did y'all have a good time?" "It was good seeing them, we did a lot of women's stuff, you know, shopping, the nail tech, by the way, do you like my nails?" "Oh, yeah, they're cute." "I had my toes done too, look." I see, I see, now enough of the small talk, shower, and meet me in the bedroom." I said with a smirk on my face. "For real, it's only 7 pm?" "I don't care about the time, Mr. Willie wants to play," I said with a big ass smile on my face. "Oh, he does, huh, okay, okay, I did promise and whatever Mr. Willie wants he is going to get, meet you in the shower, honey," Laquita said as she grabbed my package and pulled me in her direction. "Well damn, say no more," I said.

That night Laquita and I tore the damn room up and all the sheets were on the floor, my underwear on the lamp, and her panties were on the other side of the room. It's always a pleasure to please my wife in bed. She pleases me and I return, I give her Mr. Willie, ha, ha.

As I mentioned earlier, it wasn't always like that. Now, let me fill you in on some juicy details.

♠

SPADE

2

PAST DATING ISSUES

IN THE PAST:

"Laquita, one day, you're going to be my wife." "Brent, one day you will forget all about me." "No, you're wrong, you will be my wife." "Well, I guess then, you'll be my husband," Laquita said with a smile on her face.

I still remember saying those words to Laquita around the time we both graduated from high school. I knew this would be a test for our relationship because we were headed to separate colleges for a while.

TWO HEARTS, TWO SOULS, ONE LIFE

For our freshmen year in college, we rarely saw each other and when we did, we made the best of it. We saw each other on Christmas and Thanksgiving as we enjoyed our families. In our sophomore year, that's when everything went downhill. Laquita was starting to take her studies very seriously and she rarely had time for me. At the time, I didn't understand it because I was in love with her and I wanted us to be together. The walls came crashing down on me one day when she and I were conversing on the phone.

"Look, I 'm not trying to stress you out at all, but I just want to see you and hear from you more." "I can't right now, my studies are very important to me." Even more important than me?" "At this moment, I am afraid so, I mean, not that way, but my studies need extra attention, I have to take them seriously if I want to graduate with honors." "With honors, so I am not important anymore?" "I didn't say that, look, you should be taking your studies seriously also, I am not downing you, but if I am to become a doctor, I have to study, I don't have time for anything else, you have to understand that, don't you?" "Oh yeah, I understand all right, you go and do your studies, our relationship isn't that important, do you, I am good." "You are good, is that all you got from this conversation, well guess what, I am good too." "Okay then, bye," I said loudly. "Bye," Laquita said as she hung the phone up in my ear. I could hear her struggling to hang up the phone, so I just pushed the hang-up button, and tears came down my face.

I was hurt, I never thought we would break up, I just thought we could work through anything.

IN THE PAST:

"Dad, how do you know when you're in love?" "Why are you asking that son, you do know you're a little too young to be falling in love?" "I know, but I am just curious." "It's a different feeling for everyone, but the way I knew I was in love with your mother, is that I was tired of seeing other women, and I realized my life wasn't complete without her, I didn't want to live without her, when you ever get to that point you will know, but always remember this son, if a woman loves you, no matter what happens in your life, she'll either stay with you and never leave you, or one day, she'll come back to you, that's if she ever leaves you, do you understand?" "I think so, Dad, why is love so complicated?" "It's not son, people make it complicated, remember this also, let a woman find her place in your life and while she does, just play your position, that's how real relationships work, you get it?" "I guess, but how do I let a woman know her place?" "Hey, I didn't say anything about you letting her know anything, she's the woman, she will know, as far as your position, just be the man, she can lean on and turn to, capeesh?" "Okay, Dad," I said as I was still puzzled about the whole love thing.

I still remembered that talk with my Dad even though Laquita and I were broken up. "Brent, what's wrong, aren't you going to the party in the west dorm?" My best friend Steven said. "No man, I am staying here to study, I have a big exam at the end of the week." "Say, what, you're turning down a party, what's wrong did, Laquita dump your ass?" I immediately started tearing up. "Whoa, oh hey, man, I was just kidding, what's with the tears, Brent?"

"Laquita and I did break up." "Wait, what, why?" "She's busy with schoolwork, she's too busy for me now." "Say what, are you sure she's not dating one of those football jocks?" "Hell no, I mean, I don't think so." "That's got to be it, schoolwork and studies shouldn't be more important than love, right?" "No, it shouldn't." "My brother, you know what you should do?" "No, what?" "You should start dating other girls, man, you shouldn't be crying over puppy love, you're a man, now come on, and let's go mingle," Steven said. I wasn't feeling the mingling thing or talking to other girls as he was saying, but I felt it was best I get out of my dorm room and try to have some fun.

"Come on man. Hurry up." Steven said as I grabbed my jacket and ran out of the room. The party was jumping, and I reluctantly exchanged numbers with about four pretty girls. "Man, see, I knew you could do it." "Do what, you kept bringing girls over to me and lying." "Lying, so what, what's a little white lie, anyway." "You telling those girls that my Dad is a multimillionaire, is stretching it a bit, isn't it?" "Brent stop being so uptight, it worked didn't it, besides, you need to get over Laquita." He said but I just acted like I didn't hear him. "Who said that I wanted to get over Laquita?" I whispered to myself.

CHARLES LEE ROBINSON JR.

When I got back to my room, I looked through my phone and deleted those girls' phone numbers. As I sat by myself, something came over me. It was like a little voice saying, "Call Laquita." So, I did, and each time the phone just rang and rang. I hung up the damn phone because I felt like an idiot especially after deleting those girls' phone numbers.

Those were the loneliest days. It taught me a lesson. I realized how much I missed her, and I also had more time to do my studies. We were both heading to our last year in college, and it was around Thanksgiving. We both went home to be with our families, and that's how we started dating again.

It was like a mutual thing. We locked eyes with each other, and we approached each other down the sidewalk. After talking to her and explaining my perspective, I gained a deeper understanding of her drive. She told me that she understands I just wanted us to spend more time together. We hugged and kissed. It felt like we never broke up or were apart for as long as we were. Our chemistry was powerful, so it was easy for us just to pick up where we left off.

TWO HEARTS, TWO SOULS, ONE LIFE

♠

SPADE

3

OUR MARRIAGE WAS ATTACKED

"Good evening, Dr. Spade," I said as I walked into the house. "Stop being funny, Mr. Spade. "What, you are a doctor, aren't you?" "Well, yes, I am, and I am your wife. Why don't you say good evening, baby, or how was your day, honey?" "Okay, honey, baby, doctor, ha, ha." "Bae, stop it, I had a hard day at work." "Okay, okay, so did I. Do you want to talk about your day, and maybe get a foot rub?" "Oh, you know exactly what momma wants, don't you?" "Yes, I do, and daddy is here to please." "Ooh, daddy, let me get out of these clothes and shower first. "Okay, I am right behind you."

As Laquita went up to shower, I walked into the kitchen and thought to myself. Our conversation could have gone a different way, but one thing I've learned about my wife is that she loves it when you listen to her. She loves the attention, and when I'm attentive, she melts in my arms, causing me to melt into hers. I pay attention and I always ask her how her day was. I love her and I want to make sure she's all right. When she's happy, the whole house is happy.

After Laquita was out of the shower, I got in and turned the water on hot. After a hard day of work, a good shower always hits the spot. Sometimes, I find myself in a corner in the shower and put my head down, and just let the hot water run all down my body. It's a mental meditation for me, and I think and I pray for my wife and me. Believe me, it's much needed these days.

I finished my shower and listened to my wife tell me about her whole day. After our talk was over, I pulled her over to my shoulder and then placed her beautiful face on my chest, and I told her, "Baby, it will be okay." I kissed her on the forehead, and we lay down and went to sleep.

CHARLES LEE ROBINSON JR.

My alarm went off that morning, and it was time to go to work and do it all over again. "Have a good day, honey," I said as I made my way off to work. I work for the Shelton and Sheldon Law Firm in downtown Rochester, New York.

The office is always stressful because it has at least ten young lawyers working there, and six of them are women. Most of the day, they are in and out of my office, especially Danyele Tatum. I believe the young lady has a crush on me. I try my best to stay away from her, but she always finds a way to try to get into my space.

"Mr. Spade, I have some juicy gossip for you." Miss Hampton said. "Miss Hampton, you are a lawyer; what are you gossiping about?" "So, what does that have to do with it, Mr. Spade? Now, do you want to hear the juicy gossip or not?" "I guess, what is it?" "You know Miss hot ass Danyele?" "Of course, I know her; she works here." "Anyhow, she's been telling everyone on the job that she has a crush on you." "What is that woman crazy, I am a married man, for crying out loud." "Well, apparently she doesn't care, all I'm saying is, you better watch out." "Watch out for what, I love my wife, I don't want her." "Well, whatever you do, don't do a luncheon with her, she might slip you a mickey and make you do a quickie, ha, ha." She chuckled. "Ha, ha, you are so funny, Miss Hampton, is she telling people that for real?" I whispered. "For real, I am telling you, you better be careful, are you going to tell your wife?" "Uhm, well, let me handle this." "Okay then, ooh, look at the time, I have to meet a client way on the other side of town," She said as she hurried out of the office.

Just as Miss Hampton left my office, Danyele walked by with a tight-fitting dress on and winked at me. I hurried and locked my door while placing my head in my hands. Man, oh man, this shit is crazy. People have no respect for married folks these days.

Weeks and weeks went by, and Danyele kept on trying to get my attention. Up until that point, I hadn't told Laquita, but one day after she got home from work, I had to say to her.

"Honey, listen, we need to talk." "Yes, we do, can I please go first?" "But, Laquita, I have something serious to talk to you about." "Please, let me go first, please, this is weighing on my chest." She said as she put her right hand over her heart. "Damn, this sounds serious, okay, mine can wait, you go first." "Thank you, where do I start?" She said as her forehead started to perspire.

"Listen, I feel I have to tell you this, no, I need to tell you this because you are my husband and I can't hold this inside." "Hold what? What's going on?" "Well, I didn't want to tell you this because I don't want any problems." Now, I am getting worried, what problems?" "It's this doctor at the hospital who has a crush on me, and he keeps asking me out to dinner. I've told him over and over that I am happily married." "Wait, what, I'll kill him," "No, Brent, no, I can't lose my job, I will get this under control." "No, I am your husband, and we will get this under control, what's his name, did you tell your H.R. Department, this is harassment or something, isn't it?" "Yes, it is harassment because I don't want that man, and he just keeps trying to tell me what he can do for me." "This is bullshit, honey, if you don't handle this, I will, what's his name?" "Brent, honey, no." "I said what's this bitch boy's name?" "Dr. Darrel Crenshaw, that's his name," Laquita said as she put her hand on her hips while trying to control tears and a runny nose. "Calm down, honey, I will let you handle this," I said just to put her heart at ease because deep down this bitch boy was going to see me.

After Laquita calmed down a bit and wiped her face, she turned to me and said, "Now you can tell me what you wanted to talk about before I went rambling on about what's going on with me." My mind was racing like a Kentucky Derby stallion because I was enraged by what my beautiful wife had just told me. My body was trembling like Fall leaves blowing off trees, but I knew I had to calm myself down before I told her. It was ironic in a way that we were both going through the same situations. This made it easier for me to tell Laquita what was going on because she was a genuine person, one who would tell me the truth about her situation.

"Bae, tell me, you're scaring me by being silent and just pacing in a half circle. "I know, I was just taken aback by what I just heard." "I know it is a lot to take in, but let me handle it like you said, please don't do anything crazy." "Crazy, I won't." "Do you promise?" She said, but I ignored her request. I started to tell her about Danyele, and she instantly forgot about the promise I had made.

"This bitch said what, oh hell no, she is going to get a beat down." "Hold up, calm down, calm down." "How ARE YOU TELLING ME TO CALM DOWN?" She yelled. "Honey, honey, take a deep breath and calm down, no yelling, I will handle this, I got this." "You better, because if you don't handle this, Dr. Laquita Spade will," she said in anger. "Oh, so now she's Dr. Spade?" I said under my breath, "What did you say?" "Oh, nothing, I was just talking to myself." "Oh, about handling this situation?" "Yes, yes," I said as I wiped the sweat off my forehead.

I grabbed Laquita's arm gently, looked into her eyes, and said, "I love you and I won't let any harm come to you, you are my responsibility, and as your husband, I will honor whatever you say, especially in this situation." "I know, Bae, and in the return, I feel the same way, but if you can't handle this little bitch, I will pull the weave or sew end out of her damn head, she does have weave right." "Yes, I guess a little, but honey, honey, ha, ha, no need for that." "My place as your wife is to hold us down in ways that I know how and I will be damned if a little trifling bitch is trying to come on to my husband and try to ruin his career, let me calm down, you handle that situation and I will handle mine." She said, and we hugged each other tightly.

CHARLES LEE ROBINSON JR.

We both showered, and then we went to bed. I lay on my side of the bed with my eyes wide open. I know Laquita wanted me to promise that I would not do anything, but my mind wouldn't let that be possible. Instead she wanted me to or not, I was going to see and put an end to this punk ass, bitch boy, doctor, who was trying to approach my wife.

I let the situation breathe for a few days, and at the end of the week, I dressed up in my jogging clothes, wearing a black hoody, and went jogging near Highland Hospital, where Laquita worked. I discovered while conducting some detective work that this doctor jogs at a nearby park called Highland. I am a lawyer, of course, this bitch boy was going to get found.

I did at least two and a half laps around until I saw this guy in a green and black workout shirt with black leggings and track pants. It was Dr. Darrel Crenshaw, and he was a slender man. I approached him as he walked near me and I co-cocked his ass, I mean I punched his ass so hard he hit the ground. I got on top of him, and I hit him two more times on each side of his head. He was startled, and dazed as I stopped breathing heavily and I said, "Leave my damn wife alone do you hear me." "Who's your wife? I don't know your wife." He mumbled. "Did you hear me, leave her alone?" "I'm sorry, I'm sorry, I don't know who your wife is, but I will stop, I will stop," "What do you mean, are you fucking with a lot of married women at this hospital that you don't know?" "I am sorry, I don't know who your wife is, but I will stop."

"You better, or next time you will have more than a swollen eye." "Okay, okay." He said while panting. I hurried up and got off him because I saw a few runners down the other path, jogging. As I raised, I warned Dr. Darrel once more, "Leave my fucking wife alone, you hear me, bitch boy?" "I will, whoever she is, I promise." He said, and I fled.

As I looked back, I could see those two joggers helping him up, and I could vaguely hear them asking him if he was okay. After that, I heard him say, "I'm okay, I must have fallen, a squirrel ran out in front of me, and I fell and hit my face on that tree."

I made it back to my car and drove back home. "Hey, Bae, where have you been?" Laquita asked as I walked into the house. "Hey, you're home, uhm, I just went for a much-needed jog, hey, what happened to your hand, it looks bruised?" I asked. "Oh, this, I went out shopping and I guess I slightly slammed the door on my hand." "You guess, you either know or not, does it hurt?" "I mean, yeah, I did slightly slam it in the car door, it will be okay, it just hurts a little." "Honey, you better put some ice on it to keep it from swelling, damn how did you do that?" "Okay, get some ice. I guess I was thinking about something else while I was putting a few groceries in the car, I wasn't looking, and there you have it." "Honey, that does seem like you, you are always aware, anyway, let's get you some ice on this hand," I said as I helped my wife. While I was helping her with her hand, I couldn't but think about the ass whooping I put on that bitch boy. Hopefully, he didn't figure out who I was because Laquita will be so upset, and I don't want her to lose her job. That's all I could think about while I wrapped her hand, and I laid an ice pack on it. I finally stopped thinking about his ass because I had to make sure my wife was okay.

Laquita and I conversed some more that day, and sleep found us early Sunday evening. I woke up to the sound of my alarm clock, and it was time for work again. I arrived at the office about fifteen minutes early. As soon as I walked into my office, I was approached by that gossiping Miss Hampton.

"Mr. Spade, I heard Miss Hottie Danyele called in this morning. I guess she was attacked or something near her home." "Attacked, what do you mean attacked?" "Somebody beat her ass, is what I am hearing." "Who would do such a thing?" "That bitch probably deserved it; she needs to stop sleeping with everybody's man." She whispered. "That's not right, but damn, was she attacked, in her home or what?" "And, her messing with other people's husbands ain't right either, but she still manages that, I think Mr. Sheldon said she will be out all week." "Wow, that's crazy, keep me posted." "I will, have a good day, Mr. Spade." Miss Hampton said with a smirk on her face.

I don't know why she was smirking like that, but this was no laughing matter. Someone could have killed Danyele in that attack. This world and these people are crazy. Shortly after Miss Hampton left, I got on the phone with my client. The work was overwhelming, so the day passed quickly. As I was heading home, I decided to stop at the flower shop to get Laquita some flowers. I went and picked out her favorite, some long-stemmed, red roses. When I got home, I gave them to her, and she was delighted. "Thank you, Bae, you never cease to amaze me, and you know exactly what I like." "Of course, I do, you are my wife, see, I pay attention." "Yes, you do, Bae, guess what?" "What?" "I went to work today, and that guy who was bothering me came in with a huge black eye. He was jogging, and a squirrel crossed his path, and he fell and busted his eye, but I think that's just a cover-up." Damn, a cover-up, why?" I asked, acting as if I were shocked. "That doesn't look like a swell up from a fall, that looked like somebody beat his ass," "Do you think?" "Yes, I do, and the good thing about it is he didn't say anything to me, nor did he even look my way, he stayed quiet the entire day." "Maybe he was sore or something." Maybe, but I still think someone kicked his ass, he needed it anyways, so more power to the squirrel, I know Bae, I am being a bit mean, ha, ha." "Nope, not at all, maybe he just got what he deserved, but you know what, it's a funny thing." "What's a funny thing?" "You know that young lawyer, I told you about?" "The little bitch at your job that has a crush on you?" "Yeah, that's her, well, she was attacked by her house." "What, oh my God, who would do such a thing?" "I don't know, but I heard she won't be at work for at least a week." "Wow, that's scary. Do you think she's okay?" "I am not sure." "Well, maybe somebodies wife beat her ass from trying to fuck their husband." "Yes, maybe, but you can't take the law into your own hands," I said, and then I felt guilty for punching Dr. Darrel in the face. I paused for a second after thinking about it. "Bae, are you okay?" "Yes, just thinking about how crazy this world is." That is, well, I hope she's okay." Me too, so how is the hand?" It's better." "You know what's funny?" "What's that?" "You let me take care of you and your hand as if I were the doctor, ha, ha." "Ha, ha, I sure did, and you did a great job." She said as she chuckled. "How is that hand?" "Not that bad, why?" "What do you mean, why?" Mr. Willie is talking to you." "Oh, is he? It's a funny thing, y'all both sound alike." She said as she giggled. "How about you and I take a hot shower and go at it?" "I like the way you think, Mr. Spade." "Meet you upstairs, honey." "Oh, yes, come on, Mr. Willie." She said as we headed upstairs, and I stayed close behind.

That night, I let Laquita ride Mr. Willie, and he enjoyed every bit of it. Ecstasy took over us both as we made love for hours. The caressing of her breast, kissing her nipples, rubbing on her soft flesh, from her ass to her thighs, we were both on cloud nine. We didn't have a care in the world about all the issues that were going on; we just enjoyed each other, and that's what a husband and wife should do: listen to each other, communicate more, and love the hell out of one another.

TWO HEARTS, TWO SOULS, ONE LIFE

After we were done, I turned to her as she collected her breathing, and I said, "I love you, Miss Spade." I love you also, Mr. Spade." "Good night, honey." "Good night, bae." She said, and we fell asleep.

♠

SPADE

CHARLES LEE ROBINSON JR.

A **WOMAN'S** PLACE

4

MY CONFESSION

"Hey, Laquita, how are you doing?" "Hey Tasha, hey Kemberley, where are Portia and Sabrina?" I said. "They should be coming behind me," Kemberley said. "They better hurry up, you know produce goes quickly here at the public market, girl." I said, "I know, that's why I got up early," Tasha said. "You know those hussies are always late, hell, I will be surprised if they're not late to their own funerals," Kemberley said.

"Well, they are sisters, and twins at that," I said. "I wonder why their momma didn't name identical twins, Mandy and Sandy, why the hell Portia and Sabrina, ha, ha," Tasha said. "Hush up, hush, here they come." Kemberley said in a whisper, and a chuckle followed. "Hey girls, so y'all husbands let y'all out this morning?" Portia said as she walked up. "It's good to see my girls early this morning." Sabrina said as she walked up." "Husband lets us, hell, Brent knows where I am going at all times," I said. "At all times, he got your ass tamed, doesn't he?" Portia said. "Portia, stop starting trouble," Sabrina said. "That hussy is just mad because she doesn't have a husband," Tasha said. "I am not mad, I am happily divorced," Portia said with a smile on her face.

"Now, who in the hell says they're happily divorced?" Kemberley asked. "Exactly," I said as we started walking and headed toward the produce section. "Damn, it's a lot of people here already, and we are here early. Tasha said. "Anyways, my husband, Michael, is always aware of my whereabouts," Kemberley said. "Jordan always knows where his sexy wife is, and that's two places, getting money and shopping, ha, ha," Tasha said.

"She already knows how I roll with my boo, Jimmy, my fine ass husband never has a problem about where I go," Sabrina said. "That's because his ass is pussy whipped," Portia said and we all laughed. "Whatever, girl, you're a hater." "I ain't hating shit, you're my twin, y'all hussies know I am just messing with y'all, damn lady, push me the fuck over," Portia said as a young lady nudged her as she passed by.

TWO HEARTS, TWO SOULS, ONE LIFE

"Look, don't you start no mess here in this Public Market, I don't want to kick someone's ass," I said. "Speaking of kicking ass, why is your hand wrapped up?" Sabrina asked. "Girl, if they disrespect, I will go for their neck, period," Portia said. "Ha, ha, that girl is crazy as hell," Kemberley said in laughter. "Oh, my hand, it's a long story," I said with hesitation. "Okay we have time, let's sit in the food court, I want to hear this shit," Tasha said. "I know, right?" Portia said. "Oh, this sounds like it will be juicy," Sabrina said.

We all sat down on some benches located near the hot dog stands, and I began to tell them about what truly happened to my hand. "Bitch, you did what?" Portia yelled. "Be quiet, hush, shh, be quiet, please. "I said. "Laquita, tell me you didn't beat that young lawyer's ass," Tasha said in a low tone. "That's what I'm talking about, she shouldn't be trying to screw someone else's husband," Kemberley said. "I did, she left me no choice," I said. "Now, this shit is juicy, woo, woo," Sabrina said as she pumped her fist in the air. "You are crazy, you are putting your life in jeopardy for some dick?" Portia said. "Hell no, I am putting my life on the line for my husband and my marriage, and the crazy thing is, I will do it again," I said.

"Now this is some craziness, you love Brent that much, huh?" Sabrina said. "I sure do, and I love the life we've made for each other, so if anybody thinks they can come between my husband and me, oh, bitch, it's a problem." I said, "Problemo." Tasha yelled out in laughter. "Girl, hush, before we get kicked out of the Public Market, ha, ha,"

Kemberley said. "Hell, my twin, almost did that, starting trouble and shit with that lady who nudged her ass," Sabrina said with a chuckle. "Well, she shouldn't have tried to knock me down, but back to Miss Tyson over here, you knocked that bitch out, didn't you? Portia said." "I sure the hell did, and I messed up my hand in the process, and the funny thing is, Brent noticed my hand being bruised and he offered to take care of it," I said. "Ha, ha, like he was the damn doctor and not you," Tasha said. "That's right, ha, ha, he was so cute in doing it too," I said. "If Brent ever finds out, girl, you're in a world of trouble," Kemberley said. "He won't find out, and none of y'all better not utter a word, so promise me," I said forcefully.

They all promised, and since we were hungry, we ordered some food and conversed a little more. "I remember the last time we were together; you were telling us about how you and Brent met and the things you guys have been through to get to this point, you truly love that man," Portia said as she took a bite out of her hot dog. "Yes, I do, and I also know my place in our marriage," I said. "Your place, what do you mean your place?" Portia said, her face all scrunched up. "Knowing your place in a relationship or a marriage isn't a bad thing," I said. "I don't know about this place shit, no man better not tell me to know my place," Tasha said as she took a bite from her pizza. "Y'all chicks are dumb, I also know my place, and it doesn't have anything to do with what my husband says or thinks," Sabrina said. "Sabrina, you know exactly what I'm talking about, you see, I know my place in my marriage and I know my husband's position, and that's how we work out so well, I am his wife, I am his helper as God said in the Bible, my place as a woman and his wife, is how I can keep everything in sync with him and us as a whole," I said. "That shit sounds confusing but okay, so you're saying, he's not telling you what your role should be, you just know it as a woman?" Portia asked. "That's sort of it, if you want to put it that way," I said. "I never felt that way in my marriage; we just get along," Tasha said. "Do you and your husband argue a lot?" Sabrina asked Tasha. "Yeah, we do," Tasha said. "It's okay to debate, but if the two of you argue a lot, it may be because you don't know your place with him, and he doesn't know his position in y'all's marriage. It's obvious he loves you because he's still with you," I said. "I guess you're right, but we always have sex after, and then everything is okay," Tasha said. "Ha, ha, this girl is stupid, I'm glad I know my place," Kemberley said. "You do, and what is that?" Portia asked. "Face down and ass up, that's my place and that's my husband's favorite position, ha, ha," Kemberley said, and we all started laughing until tears came falling. "I know that's right, ha, ha," Sabrina said as she giggled.

We ate our food and split up for a while to get everything that they wanted, except for Portia and me. She was more inquisitive, and I believe it was because her marriage had ended in failure. She kept asking me the same questions over and over again. Finally, after we stopped in an area by the apples and the oranges, she asked me a question I wasn't ready for.

"Laquita, you and Brent seem to have yall shit together, I mean y'all marriage is tight, has anyone of you guys cheated on each other?" "Why would you ask that?" "The reason is that my husband cheated on me, and I just couldn't get over it. I even cheated on him to get him back, but that never helped me resolve the problem of why he decided to do what he did."

"So, you both cheated on each other?" "Yes, shit, he did it first," "Well, I am the last person who should be telling you this because two wrongs don't make it right." "I know, you're right because I felt like shit after I slept with Zeek." "You slept with Zeek, you mean Alonzo Evans, what, damn," I said, surprisingly. "Yes, I did, it was short-lived, but it was good, he went his way and I went my way shortly after, we only slept together one time." "Wow, you and Zeek, I would've never guessed that, but to answer your question, I did cheat on Brent one time." "What, you did, does he know?" "Of course not." "Do you think he ever cheated on you?" "Truthfully, I don't know, but if he did, he was good at it, and you know, usually we women are better at it, so I don't know, I never thought about it because Brent has always been good to me." "That's good, but that doesn't mean he didn't; you just never found out." "Could be, but I don't want to find out, I do know this, he loves me, if he did cheat on me, it would've probably been years ago when we were going through difficult issues, we were just getting to know one another." "For your sake, I hope so, because if his ass is cheating now, we both going to fuck him up, ha, ha." "Yeah, that part," I said as I pointed my finger at Portia.

While we were still on the subject, the rest of the girls came around with bags full of food. "Hey, what's up, girls? Look at all this stuff. I think we should do some real shopping now," Tasha said as she looked at our bags. "Tasha, that is a good idea, girl," Kemberley said. "I need some more shopping therapy, yes, plus it's this Canary dress I want, it's at Tiffany's Boutique," Sabrina said. "That high-ass store, with all that bougie shit, you can have that shit," Portia said. "You are just cheap, shut up girl, and go buy those damn hammy-downs at the Salvation Army, ha, ha," Sabrina said with laughter.

We all started laughing as we headed out of the public market. Kemberly walked up to Sabrina and said, "Are you sure you guys are twins?" We all started laughing even harder. "By the way, I ain't cheap, I am smart," Porta said to Sabrina. "Yes, it is sad to say that she's my twin, and identical at that. I like rich things, and she likes to buy cheap clothing. hell, who do you know that makes 80 grand more a year and still wants to live in the hood?" Sabrina said. "For your information, I don't live in the hood, I live on Norton Street near Irondequoit," Portia said. "Do you live in Irondequoit, no, all you have to do is walk down the street and your ass is getting shot at, that's why I moved out to Penfield, I love my life," Sabrina said. "Bougie, bitch shut up," Portia said. "Okay, twins, stop the bickering, let's go shopping, plus I want to fill y'all in on something that I was just about to tell Portia about," I said. "I am not thinking about Sabrina," Portia said. "I love you too," Sabrina said. "Will y'all kiss and hug with y'all petty asses," Kemberley said.

They both gave Kemberley a mean look and rolled their eyes. "You guys are a trip, now let's go shopping," Tasha said. "You took the words right out of my mouth, now let go," I said, and we got into our cars and we headed to Eastview Mall out in Victor, New York.

SPADE

5

MY RELATIONSHIP WAS TESTED

We made it to the mall and we parked near the food court. "Hey, let's get something to eat," Tasha said. "Damn, girl, didn't we just eat at the Public Market?" Portia asked Tasha. "Whatever," Tasha said. "Whatever, hell, that's why your damn hips are spreading," Portia said. "No, that's because I'm getting dick, and you're not," Tasha said. "Girl, whatever, dick doesn't make you spread like that, it's those hamburgers, steaks, and french fries, you've been eating," Portia said, and we all laughed. "Stop being rude to one another I said. "No, let them keep on, this is for our amusement," Sabrina said. "Hell, I'm hungry also and I get plenty of a ding-a-ling," Kemberley said. "Ha, ha, this girl old as hell still calling a dick, a ding-a-ling," Portia said. "I call it what I want to call it, at least I am getting some, ding-a-ling, that is," Kemberley yelled out. "Girls, keep it down, they are going to kick us out of this mall," I said. "Let's stop all the bullshitting, and let's get some food and then we can listen to what Laquita has to tell us," Sabrina said as we entered the Steak House Restaurant's entrance.

After our meal, I started telling the girls one of my most closely guarded secrets, because sometimes people think you live in a perfect relationship when, in fact, a relationship isn't perfect at all; it consists of two people who never give up on each other, despite the hurt and pain.

IN THE PAST:

Our breakup phone call…I will never forget it!

"Look, I 'm not trying to stress you out at all, I just want to see you and hear from you more." "I can't right now, my studies are very important to me." Even more important than me?" "At this moment, I am afraid so, I mean, not that way, but my studies need extra attention, I have to take them seriously if I want to graduate with honors." "With honors, so I am not important anymore?" "I didn't say that, look, you should be taking your studies seriously also, I am not downing you, but if I am to become a doctor, I have to study, I don't have time for anything else, you have to understand that, don't you?" "Oh yeah, I understand all right, you go and do your studies, our relationship isn't that important, do you, I am good." "You are good, is that all you took from this conversation? Well, guess what, I am good too." "Okay then, bye," I said loudly. "Bye,"

"That was the conversation that took me over the edge," I said. "Damn, I know you were angry, I mean he couldn't understand where you were coming from, hell, look at you now, you are a doctor for crying out loud?" Tasha said. "At the time, I guess he didn't," I said. "Okay, I bet he realizes it now, y'all are still together and happily married, right?" Sabrina said. "He knows, and I know better now, and we are both happy. It takes two people who are happy with themselves first, and then they can build a happy marriage and hopefully live happily ever after," I said. "You said hopefully," Portia said. "Hey, you never know what can go wrong, but for Brent and me, we understand what it takes to keep our marriage going, but will y'all let me tell the damn story?" I said with a smirk on my face. "Let her tell it, let her tell it," Kemberley shouted out.

"As I was saying, that was the conversation that did it for me, because here I was trying to work on a career that could not only take care of myself but my partner also, I guess I felt like he was being so selfish, even though, I hung up on Brent that night, we never officially broke up, I was hurt, so I dived, deep into my work for a while, but then there came a time when I got lonely and that's when I met this guy named, Adam Berman, he was one of my classmates and he also was studying to be a doctor."

IN THE PAST:

I was walking out of class, and as I was leaving, I bumped into this tall, handsome young man who was entering the classroom as I was walking out. "Oh, excuse me, I am sorry, I didn't mean to bump into you." He said. "It's okay, you didn't hurt me or anything, are you okay? We did collide pretty hard." "Well, your head is kind of hard, ha, ha, no, I am just playing, just playing," He said as he waved both hands in the air as if he was surrendering, *"Big head, huh, that was cute, I needed that laugh, thank you." "You're welcome, by the way, my name is Adam Berman." "Nice to meet you, Adam Berman. Will you be in this class? That's why I am here to talk to the professor, I will be taking the same class you are taking now, so what's your name?" "I am Laquita, Laquita Sharpe." "Well, Laquita Sharpe, looks like we will be sharing this class." "I guess so, it was nice talking to you, but I must get to my next class." "Okay, talk to you soon,"* Adam said.

"So, you started talking to this Adam guy, and you and Brent were freshly broken up, I guess our girl isn't a little angel like we thought," Kemberley said. "It wasn't even like that, I mean, Brent and I hadn't spoken for about a month at the time, and truthfully, I thought we would never talk again," I said. "You were vulnerable and you had to do what you had to do, yeah, I do remember fine ass Adam, girl," Tasha said with excitement.

"Tasha, stop it," I said. "I mean yeah, damn, he was cute, your ass was slick then because I never knew and I was right there in college with you," Tasha said with sarcasm. "Your nosy ass wasn't supposed to know, that's why you didn't know, continue with the story, I want to hear the juicy shit," Portia said. "Whatever, I was there and I knew Adam, Laquita should have said something," Tasha said. "Why because you were lusting him but he was interested in your girl here,

Laquita, ha, ha, your ass is slick girl, high five," Portia said with crazy, wild laughter. I reluctantly gave her a high five. "Listen, I was still in my feelings, and I was hurt from my last conversation with Brent, plus I didn't want anyone to know we weren't talking anymore," I said. "When did you give him that kitty cat, meow, ha, ha?" Kemberley asked as she giggled. "Now, that's what I want to know," Portia said.

"Well, Adam and I started doing homework and studying together. I was lonely, and I was vulnerable, plus Brent had stopped calling me and texting me, so my emotions took over one night." "Your emotions hell, bitch you were horny," Tasha said. "Shut up, hoe, so that we can hear her story. This is getting juicy as hell," Portia shouted. "Your momma's a hoe." Tasha said to Portia, "Hey, my momma's not a hoe, Sabrina said as she had been quiet and just listening to me tell my story the whole time. "Bitch go back to sleep, you haven't said one damn word all this time, now you want to say something," Tasha said. "Tasha, chill out, now apologize," I said. "Apologize, why should I apologize, Portia always starts shit with me," Tasha said. "I don't ever bring your alcoholic momma in it," Portia said. "Ladies. Ladies, do y'all want to hear the rest of my story or not?" I asked. "See, see, and you want me to apologize?" Tasha said. "How did I get into this mess?" Sabrina asked. "Because ya'll twins and y'all have the same damn momma, are you having a blonde moment," Tasha said. "Tasha," I said. "Okay, okay, I apologize, now can you please finish, so you finally gave Adam the pussy?" Tasha said. "Damn, you are a trip, Tasha, so is that when you gave him some pussy?" Portia asked. "Yes, yes, we did it, and I cried afterward," I said. "You cried, was the ding a ling too big?" Sabrina asked. We all laughed. "No, it was just right, and it was good, but I couldn't help but think about Brent," I said. "Wait a minute, the dick was good, and you were thinking about your ex, girl are you crazy, I would've been riding that thang," Portia said. "No, you would not, that's why you're dickless right now," Tasha said. "Tasha," I yelled again. "If you don't shut this girl up," Portia said. "All right, Portia, leave it alone, now we know y'all love each other," Kemberley said. "Will you two let me finish my story?" I asked. "Okay, so what happened to this Adam guy? Did he dump you after, or did you dump him?" Sabrina asked. "He dumped you, didn't he?" Kemberley asked. "No, he did not dump me, even though he made me feel good, it's Brent whom I thought about, I felt so lonely inside. "I said. "What happened next?" Portia asked. "It was getting near the holidays, and I knew I would be going home because I've always gone home for Thanksgiving and so did Brent, so I finally told Adam I couldn't see him anymore," I said.

"You waited until you were about to go home and you told him?" Sabrina asked. "Yeah, I did, and I am not proud of it," I said. "How did he take it?" Kemberley asked. "He was hurt, I could tell," I said. "And, that's when you came home, then you and Brent started back talking?" Tasha asked. "Yes, I was so happy to see him," I said. "He didn't even know you had it planned huh?" Portia said. "Nope, but I knew I was going to get my man back," I said. "Did you ever see Adam again?" Sabrina asked. "I saw him on campus, but he stopped speaking to me," I said. "Yeah, you hurt that tall, fine, sexy man's feelings," Tasha said. "Damn, it sounds like you wanted to fuck him," Portia said. "No, no, it's not that, I was just lost in the moment," Tasha said. "Bitch, you're just lost," Portia said, and we all started laughing. "Whatever," Tasha said.

"Does Brent know that you cheated on him or slept with another man?" Kemberley asked. "No, I never told him and he doesn't need to know either," I said.

"I am glad you got your man back; I hope Brent never finds out," Portia said. "I don't think that was cheating anyways because you two weren't together," Tasha said. "If they never told each other that it was over and they slept with someone else, that is cheating in my eyes, I mean, how do we know Brent didn't cheat and fuck someone else?" Portia asked. "We don't know, and I don't care, that was so long ago, we have a wonderful marriage, and I won't ever let anything come between us," I said. "I know that's right, girl," Sabrina said.

"I will take that to the grave with me, you girls are the only ones that know, so please keep it that way," I said adamantly. "My lips are sealed," Tasha said. "Mine too," Sabrina said. "I won't say a word," Portia said. "It's locked and sealed, sis," Kemberley said.

♠

SPADE

6

SOME MEN DON'T GET IT

That evening, I arrived home a little before Laquita. Just as I was about to get into the shower, my phone rang, and it was Stanley. He kept asking me questions about women and what advice I had for him, because he said he wanted to settle down with the right woman. I thought about all the games he played with women in the past, and as a good friend, I had to be honest.

"First of all, you need to stop being a damn narcissist, and stop lying all the damn time, man." "Damn, tell me how you feel, I am not a narcissist, I am the man, so, I play my role and she should listen to me," Stanley said. "What in the hell did you say, man, don't you have two daughters?" "Yes, Jessica, and Jeanette, what do they have to do with this?" "They are young girls, and one day they will be women. How would you like it if a young man acts and treats your daughters like that?" "Treat my daughters like what, man, I will kill somebody over my daughters," Stanley said. "Exactly, see, now you need to check yourself on how you treat women because you wouldn't like it if it were done to your daughters." "Man, that's different, but my father taught me that way." "Your father came up in a different time, men were very stern then, plus women had to do what their men said back then. Women now have rights, and they are human and not to be treated like property or worse than dogs."

"I didn't know I was that bad. I thought that was what being a man was all about." "You can still be a man and still treat women with respect and dignity, look here, I promise you, it will take you a long way and you might just get that wife you've been looking for." "I will try to do better, but man, when I'm giving her back shots from the back, I have to show her who the man is, right?" "You are lame, ha, ha, of course, now being in charge in the bed is different, but even then, some women want to be in control." "Hell no, that's where I draw the damn line, I have the dick, she doesn't, she can't tell me how to give it to her." "Ease up, man, you never know, she might teach you something new." "Hell no, no woman can teach me anything in bed, you hear me?" "Yeah, I hear you, listen, I have to go, someone's calling on my other line, remember this, you need to chill out, take some of those old macho man ways out of your mind, stop being a damn caveman, women need to be treated with care, and honesty, later," I said as I hung up the phone.

CHARLES LEE ROBINSON JR.

I must admit I was a little frustrated talking to Stanley. That lame-ass thinking is one reason a lot of men are single.

I clicked over to my other line, and it was Carlos. "What's going on, Brent? Are you and Steven still talking?" "Hey Carlos, man, that dude irks my nerves sometimes." "Yeah, but y'all are like brothers." "We are, but he says and does some ignorant shit sometimes, damn this fool keeps calling me back," I said as I could see Stanley hitting me up on my other line. "Who is that, Steven?" "No, that's your lame-ass boy, Stanley, man, I can't get through to him, he doesn't know how to treat women." "I know, he doesn't believe he is a narcissist, but I've seen him with women; he has that caveman mentality." "Yes, he does, and he doesn't understand that women shouldn't be treated that way." Hey, hopefully, he finds out one day." Carlos said as he chuckled. "Yeah, when he ends up dead somewhere, and some woman is going to hang that fool by his balls." "Ha, ha, not by his balls, damn, ouch, this shit hurts just thinking about it, ha, ha." "Ha, ha, yeah, right, that got me grabbing my shit."

"Well, enough talking about that lame ass, lying ass dude, listen, Brent, I want to meet a woman like how you met Laquita, I mean I want a woman I can grow with and we can invest in one another, that's what I want." "Carlos, if that's what you want, then you have to go after it, but make sure you're ready." "Ready, what do you mean ready?" "Make sure you're not getting a woman all worked up for no damn reason." No reason, why would I do that?" "Because I saw you do it with Yvonne, she wasn't ready for a relationship, but you kept stalking her, and then when she was ready, you backed out and started dating other girls, now that's not right." "I thought I was ready, but she did stupid shit and irritated me so I changed my mind."

"Changed your mind, you can't change your mind when you made her open up to you, just to make her vulnerable and then leave her, that's not right." "You're on the outside looking in, man, it wasn't exactly like that." "Then what was it exactly like?" I asked, and Carlos just got quiet.

"Well, maybe it was but don't I have the right to change my mind especially if she's getting on my damn nerves?" "Of course, you do, but don't come after a woman you're not ready for, that's all I'm saying," I said. "Look, I am not perfect, and that's why I am asking for your advice. You and Laquita are still together, and I want to find someone that I can spend my life with, too."

"You know what my dad said to me one day?" "What does your Pops say?" "He said don't approach a woman unless you're ready to take on everything that comes with a relationship, in other words, don't poke the bear." "Your Pops is a smart man." "He is, and he taught me a lot about women and relationships. Do you want to know what else he said?" "What's that?" "He said some men don't get it." "Meaning men don't understand how to treat a woman?" "Sort of, but I took it as most men don't know their position in a relationship and some think everything should be as they say, that's wrong, you'll see when you understand your position and you know a woman's place without the two of you even talking about it, that's when everything flows smoothly and you both give the relationship time to grow and flourish into something special." "Damn, now you're getting too deep on me, I can't comprehend that shit, you know I only went to the tenth grade, ha, ha." "Man, you're dumb just like Stanley, ha, ha." "Don't say that I know what you're saying, I am just messing with you." "Yeah, right, so what do I mean?" "You're saying you're the dominant one in the relationship, and the woman should know her role."

"You are just as stupid as Stanley; don't you have three sons at home?" "Yes, I do, Jacob, Mason, Carlos Jr., you know that." "Exactly, I know that, I just hope they get some become aware one day and I hope they don't think a man should always be the head over a relationship or household," "They will be just like their Daddy." Then God help them, man, I have to go, I think Laquita just pulled up." "I am teaching my sons to be men," Carlos said. "Whatever, yeah, cavemen, ha, ha," I said as I hung up the phone.

All I could do was nod my head. I couldn't believe the conversations I had with two of the men I hang out with. It's disheartening to realize that some men don't understand. One thing I learned is that those men don't have to get it, but I will. I admire and cherish my wife, and I know what it takes to keep her, and I will do my damnest to please her and treat her like a woman is supposed to be treated. "Hey, honey, how was your day?" I asked as Laquita walked in the door. I could tell she was very exhausted. I watched her put her bags down, and she plopped down on the sofa. I quickly sat right beside her and placed my head on her shoulder, and I caressed her arms and legs. Right then, I knew it was time to ask my wife how her day was, and I was all ears to what she had to say. I must pay attention.

CHARLES LEE ROBINSON JR.

SPADE

7

MAKING SURE MY WIFE IS PLEASED

"Bae, I had a long day, and it was stressful, and I couldn't wait for it to end." "It was that bad, Dr. Spade?" "Bae, I am not playing with you, what I told you about that doctor mess?" "I don't know why you don't like hearing that from me, but enough about that, honey. So, your day was stressful, huh?" I asked as I stood up, and I massaged her shoulders. "Yes, it was, ah, ah, that feels good." "That's good, ooh, you're tight right here." Yes, that's my bad shoulder, oh yeah, right there." She said.

I sat there and listened to my wife recount her day for an hour and a half. I was attentive, and I was ready to ask and answer any questions at the drop of a dime. I know Laquita had to get a lot off her chest, especially if she said she had a long and stressful day. That means prepare to listen to your wife, or else - and we all know what that 'or else' means, now don't we? "No sex! I'm just joking, no, I'm not, well maybe just a little.

Just as I was getting into massaging her back, she grabbed my hands and said, "Bae, the garage door isn't working properly, it's stuck halfway." "Again, this is the third time, and I keep paying these garage door people to fix it, and all they keep doing is taking all of my money. I'm sick of this. "Well, Bae, don't you know how to fix it yourself?" "I mean, I could, yeah, I can, but I don't have the time." "Please, Bae, please." "You mean now, now?" "Yes, it needs to be fixed, I can't keep coming home and I can't get into the garage, especially at night, somebody might grab me."

"Yeah, and if they do, I am going to hunt them down." "You'll hunt them down, Bae?" "You're damn right, but now honey, I mean I was just going to massage your entire body." "Damn, that sounds tempting but please fix that garage door before it starts getting too dark out, I promise I will make it worth your while when you're finished." "Honey, for real?" "Yes, come on now, hurry and get it done." "But I wasn't finished." "Go Bae, it's getting dark, I will have something juicy waiting for you when you're done." "Hmm, something juicy, hmmm, and wet too?" "You're so nasty, go ahead, you'll see, now let me go get into the shower."

"Can I come?" "No, the garage door please, now, go." "Do I have to?" "Bae." "Okay, okay, I am going," I said as I headed out into the garage. Truthfully, I did not want to go and fix no damn garage door, I wanted something wet and juicy because Mr. Willie was horny.

TWO HEARTS, TWO SOULS, ONE LIFE

When you love someone, you will go out of your way to make them happy. Even though I didn't want to fix that garage door, I knew it would make Laquita happy, so that's what I did. I made sure that the garage door was working before I went back into the house. Luckily, it was only off the hinges and it didn't take that long to fix.

I walked back into the house and I could hear love songs playing softly. I walked over to the bar and grabbed a bottle of wine and two glasses that were already chilled. I made my way upstairs and walked into the bedroom. Laquita was in the bathroom and I could hear her singing the lyrics to the love songs she was playing.

A thought came across my mind as I poured both glasses of wine. I decided to run downstairs and get some candles and a lighter. I wanted to make the mood romantic. I knew my wife had worked a long and stressful day and I knew as her husband it was up to me to make her forget all about her bad day. What kind of husband would I be if I didn't try to make my wife smile and be happy?

Laquita continued to sing in the shower as I lit the candles and I sat the wine and wine glasses down. At that moment, I decided to surprise my wife even more. I took all my clothes off and I walked towards the bathroom. As I stood there naked and Mr. Willie just hanging low, I walked slowly towards the shower and said softly, "Can I get in?" Then I peeped my head into the shower and pulled back the brown and gold shower curtains. "Oh, Bae, you startled me, ha, ha, sure you can get in, but the water isn't as hot as you like it, here, let me steam it up a bit," Laquita said as she turned up the temperature on the hot water faucet. "Honey, I hope it doesn't burn you," I said. "I will be okay, I will stand behind you," "I will protect you, baby," "Thank you Brent, but, ooh, do you think you can turn it down just a little bit?" She asked. "Ha, ha, you can't hang, huh, okay, I will turn it down just a little bit, but let that steam fill the room," I said as I turned to her and I gently kissed her.

"Man, you got it steamy in here, damn, Bae, you got a cute muscle ass," Laquita said as she squeezed my ass. I smiled and I said, "You like that, don't you?" "Of course, I do." She said as she squeezed my ass again. I blushed as I pulled her closer to me as the water trickled down our bodies, I grabbed her waist, my hands slid down her ass and hips, and I kissed her gently on her neck.

We had to be in the shower together for at least twenty-five minutes just to please one another. It got so hot and steamy that we both were ready to explode on one another. At that point, we didn't waste any time getting out of the steamy hot shower.

As Laquita walked into the room, she noticed the wine and the candles. I can tell she was pleased because she smiled and waltzed over to the remote control, and she turned on some good love-making music. She waltzed back over to me and her flesh and my flesh met. To her surprise, she said, "I see Mr. Willie is happy to see me once again." "Yea, look at him standing in attention," I said with a grin on my face. "Now, what does Mr. Willie want?" "Come here baby and lay in this bed and Mr. Willie will show you," I said as I pulled her gently to the bed. "Well come on Mr. Willie, my tunnel of love awaits you, and I want you to go deep," Laquita said as she whispered in my ear. "Yes, I am but first let's pose a toast, as I pour this fine wine, to get this night going." Oh, yes, I need that and I need you." I poured our glasses and we made a toast to "Love," We took a sip of our wine and Laquita walked to the side of the bed, she dropped her towel and crawled into the bed slowly, turned, and curled her finger at me to tell me to come and get it.

Of course, I wanted to please my wife, so I walked over to the bed and my tongue started working on her body as she went from a doggy position to laying on her back. I made sure my wife was pleased in every way she wanted. I understood that she had a hard day and as her husband, I wanted to take some of that burden off her, I wanted her to know that I would always have her back and I showed some of that in the way I pleased her.

What I've learned as a man is to be very attentive and willing to open up lines of communication with my wife. This is what makes our marriage that much greater, and the sex is awesome, it's on another level. Laquita and I pleased each other until we both fell asleep in the fetal position, and that's what happens when the two of you climax at the same damn time. I truly treasure my wife, and she is my rock.

CHARLES LEE ROBINSON JR.

SPADE

A **MAN'S** POSITION

8

PLAYING SPADES WITH THE FELLAS

"Bae, before you leave, don't forget it is Saturday, it's trash day, where are you headed anyway?" Laquita asked. "Damn, is it trash day again?" "Yes, Brent, now you know every weekend the trash man runs." "Yeah, right, how could I forget that? Okay, I will take it out again," I said. "You are a mess." "How am I a mess?" "How come every weekend you forget to take the trash out?" "I don't know, maybe I have better things to think about, like you," I said as I smiled. "You are certainly a sweet talker, but you better get your muscle ass and take the trash out." "Why can't women take the trash out?" "Excuse me." She said.

"Oh, nothing, I was just talking to myself, okay, I got it, honey, by the way, I am meeting the boys over at Steven's house for cards." "Okay, be safe, I guess I will hang around the house and do all the chores I couldn't do during the week." "Okay, I will see you later." She said as I walked towards the door. "Brent." "What?" "The trash," Laquita shouted, and I hurried to grab it and take it out.

TWO HEARTS, TWO SOULS, ONE LIFE

As I was driving to Steven's house, I decided to stop at the liquor store to get us something to drink. I walked into the store, and as I walked down the first aisle, I saw a woman looking for wine. She commented as I walked by her and she said, "I love when a man smells good, what is that you're wearing?" "Thank you, that must be my Creed cologne that you're smelling, it was a Christmas gift from my wife." The young woman made a fake smile and continued to look for whatever she was searching for.

I am a married man, what do I look like keeping up that kind of conversation? They won't trap me; the Devil is a lie! I bought a bottle from the top shelf, and I got the hell out of that liquor store. I never want to hurt someone I love, and that someone is my wife, Laquita. It's all about control, respect, honesty, and most of all, it's about loyalty.

I pulled up to Steven's house and I could see Carlos, Stanley, Steven, and our high college buddy Edward's car. I was somewhat shocked to see Edwards's car there, as he and Steven had a falling out over a girl named Tammy in college. As far as I know, they hadn't spoken in a few years, but I guess they made up, though. Now, this should be interesting.

I rang the doorbell, and Steven opened the screen door. "Hey, hey, guess who's here, Brent?" Steven said. "Who, Edward?" "How did you know?" Steven asked. "That bright red ass Camaro," I said. "Ha, ha, you are crazy, but yup, he's here." I whispered to Steven before I walked into the house, "I thought you two weren't cool anymore?" "We cool, hey Tammy dumped his ass too, so we are boys again." "Are you sure you can trust him?" "Yes, we are grown men now, that will never happen again, besides, we have to let that past shit go, right?" He said. "We are grown men now, I guess you're right, so who's on teams, we are playing spades, right?" I asked. "That is correct, Mr. Spade, I love saying that shit, ha, ha." "Yes, I know you do, and that is a bad joke, Mr. Ugly." I said." Oh, here we go again with that ugly shit, hey my momma said I was handsome." "Ha, ha, we all know Mrs. Tilly lied, ha, ha," I said as I laughed. "That shit isn't funny, ha, ha, come on in man so that we can whoop some ass in cards," Steven said as we walked on into the house.

"Hey, hey, the man of the hour is here," Stanley yelled while shuffling the cards. "Hey, my brother," Carlos said as he drank a shot of tequila and made the ugliest damn face while doing it.

"Well, look who it is, what cat dragged you out of the house?" Edward said. "Fellas, fellas, and Edward, what's up, the king of spades is here, what are the teams, oh hey, I brought that top-of-the-shelf shit," I said. "What's that, Henny?" "You know it," I said. "That's all these fools drink," Stanley said. "Aren't you a lawyer?" Edward asked. "Yeah, and?" "Hey, hey, that's his drink, that's his drink," Carlos shouted. "I was only asking," Edward said.

TWO HEARTS, TWO SOULS, ONE LIFE

"I know, I know, that's cool, so who's on teams, Steven, you and me against Carlos and Stanley?" I asked. "I want to play too," Edward said. "Then you have to get winners," my brother, Carlos, said. "Yeah, get winners because we are about to spank that ass, we owe them from the last time we played," Stanley said. "That's cool, I will take winners next," Edward said.

We sat down at the table and we all started talking shit while playing cards. Steven and I were kicking ass and taking names for a while until Stanley began talking shit about Edward and Steven fighting over Tammy.

"Man, shut up, I wasn't serious about that girl anyway," Steven said to Stanley. "Sure, you weren't, you're just mad because she wanted your friend, Edward," Stanley said. Just as Stanley said, Steven shot out the wrong card, and it cost us a book in spades. "Hey man, Steven, pay attention to the damn game man," I said. "I am," Steven said. "You can't be because you just cost us a damn book," I said. "Oh fuck, see man, stop talking to me about a damn girl," Steven said as a look of frustration came upon his face.

"Edward, tell us the truth, you took Mr. Ugly's girl and you gave the business," Stanley said. "Hey, don't get me involved in that shit," Edward said. They all went back and forth for about an hour and I was getting tired of hearing that shit.

CHARLES LEE ROBINSON JR.

"Will y'all play cards, damn," I yelled. "That's him," Steven said. "You're just mad, your friend took your girl," Stanley said. "Ha, ha, can we play cards man, you're a damn troublemaker," Carlos said as he poured another shot of tequila.

"Oh, shit, y'all about to be set," Stanley yelled out. "Steven, you better have another book, another spade, or something," I said. "Hey, that's called cross-boarding," Carlos said. "Man, I can only play with what's in my hand," Steven yelled. "He can't play worth shit, Carlos, we got their ass, now," Stanley said with confidence. Edward started texting on his phone.

"Hey, Edward, get ready to pick your partner, it's either one of these two bums," Stanley said. "Get their asses out of here," Carlos said. "Steven, it's on you, you better throw out something," I said as I watched Edward start texting faster on his phone.

"They set, they set," Stanley yelled as Steven shot down a damn king of spades but got beat by Stanley's queen of spades. "Hey, Edward, it's your game, you are next, my man," Carlos yelled. "Steven you should've been shot that shit out," I said and he and I got into a little spat. "Edward, so who are you picking as your partner?" I asked. "Sorry fellas, I will take a raincheck, I have to go," Edwards said. "Go, go where?" Stanley asked. "I have to go meet up with Tammy," Edwards said, and Steven's eyes got big and widened. "Tammy, not the same Tammy from school?" Steven asked. "Yeah, we still get together from time to time, and I blow her back out, but she's married, though, to this dude named Calvin," Edward said. "Damn, I thought y'all stop talking way back," Steven said. "Ha, ha, I didn't ever say that, but as I said, she's married, I just hit that when I can," Edward said.

"You don't even have the respect to not sleep with her because she's married," Steven said. "Man, fuck that shit, I don't give a damn about her husband," Edward said. "Now, that's fucked up," Stanley said as he started laughing. "That shit is messed up, you dudes ain't no good," I said. "It is what it is, I will catch you, fellas, later, I got to go and hit that," Edward said, and he left.

"Damn, that's your boy," Stanley asked Steven. "Fuck you," Steven said and he got up from the table to get a drink. "Man, what's wrong with his moody ass?" Stanley asked. "Stop acting innocent, bro." Carlos said." "What did I do?" Stanley said with sarcasm and a smile on his face. "You know what you did, that's why we lost the game because you were over there starting shit," I said.

I got up from the table and went to talk to Steven. I could tell he was still hurt by Edward still talking to a girl he once loved. I had to get him right, so I said a few things to him about life and women, and he listened.

"Steven I know you're hurt but man she wasn't worth your time anyways, she didn't care about you, so stop being upset and find someone who will love you and be loyal, and stop hanging out with a sleazeball like Edward, he doesn't have respect for himself, that's why he did that to you and you were a good friend to him, now he's sleeping with a married woman, I do not want him around me, I might just whoop his ass if he looks at Laquita any kind of way," I said.

"Hey, hey, are y'all still playing?" Carlos yelled, "Come on guys., come and get your ass kicked in spades again." Stanley yelled.

"Listen, if you want, we don't have to play anymore but remember this, if a woman wants to be kept, they won't hurt you and leave you that way, learn your position as a man, and I guarantee the next woman will think twice about leaving you," I said.

"Come, the hell on." Dr. Phil." Stanley yelled. "Man, we are coming, chill the hell out, learn my position, now how do I do that?" He asked. "Aren't you a man? Don't you know how to treat a woman?" I said. "Truthfully, I am still learning how to treat them, man, they are moody and they switch up." He said. "Women aren't that complicated if you just take your time to understand them, hell, they feel the same way about us," I said.

"That may be true, but I still don't understand their moody asses." "If you don't know now, at this age, you'll never know my brother, be willing to open up and communicate and be attentive, and when you get one make love to her as you've never done before, ha, ha, but all jokes aside with that last part, make love to their mind and you're golden, enough said, now let's go in here and get revenge on that card table," I said. "Okay, Brent, thanks for the talk. I will try to work on myself, and I will try to learn to listen to women and communicate, right?" "Right, you got it, okay, come on," I said. "All right you muthafuckas shuffle and deal the cards, we about to kick y'all asses," Steven said and we slapped hands and sat down at the card table.

We resumed the game and at the end of the night, Steven and I kicked their asses 4-1. It turned out to be a good night. Steven learned something that night, and I knew I did. I was glad I treated my woman like the queen she is and not like an asshole like Edward. I hoped that my best friend, Steven, would soon get his act together because, in the end, we all want happiness.

After defeating the boys in spades, I took my ass home. It was a little later than usual, and I knew Laquita would be worried. I tried to tiptoe into the house so I wouldn't wake her, but she was up waiting for me. "Brent, are you okay?" "Yes, honey, I am ok, just left Steven's house playing cards." "How's Steven doing?" "He's a little distraught." "Do you care to tell me?" "I'm a little tired, can we talk about it tomorrow?" "Maybe," "Maybe, why maybe?" "I might have something to do." "Something to do, huh?" "Yep, so why didn't you call me to let me know you were staying out late?" "Honestly, I lost track of time, trying to be Dr. Phil, to my messed-up friends." "You do that too, huh? For some reason, my friends think I am a relationship psychiatrist; they are too funny." "I am sorry I didn't call; I didn't mean to worry you." "Next time, can you please be a little more mindful? I thought something had happened to you." "Okay, I will, I promise, I am tired, I need to take a shower and go to bed," I said as I walked towards the stairs. "Looks like your friends wore you out, huh?" "They sure did, and boy, do they have a lot to learn." "We all do, okay, I will follow behind you." "I guess we all do, okay, why don't you walk in front of me?" "Why, Bae?" "So, I can watch all of that ass jiggle in front of me." "Ha, ha, you are so nasty, you don't want any of this good stuff." "Why is that?" "You are tired, remember?" "Damn, you're right, are you sure?" "Brent go take your shower and get your tired ass in the bed; I need to sleep also." "Okay, all right, Mr. Willie, she's rejecting us." "Ha, ha, you're a crazy man, get your butt in the shower and I will meet you in bed, Bae." I immediately smiled and ran my ass into the bathroom and I jumped into the shower. About the time I got out of the shower. I ran into the room, and Laquita was asleep. I dropped my towel and crawled my tired ass into bed. I wish I hadn't come in so late, hell, I could've gotten myself some. I pulled the covers over the bed and fell asleep. I woke up that morning feeling refreshed. I got up because I could smell the aroma of breakfast being cooked. I went downstairs, and Laquita was cooking eggs, grits, bacon, and making coffee. "Good morning, Bae, how did you sleep?" "I slept well, and you?" "It was good, I heard you snoring a little." "Was it that bad?" "No, but I could tell you were tired," Laquita said and then started finishing breakfast while I sat there and just watched. When she was finished, she spoke, "Bae, I hope you don't mind, I am going over to Tasha's house tonight, the girls and I are all meeting there for a girls' night out." "That's okay, honey, I think I am going to stay around the house and straighten up the garage and the basement some." "I cooked breakfast for you, and the coffee is made, so let me go upstairs and get dressed." "Get dressed, I thought you were going over to Tasha's house, you don't need to dress up for that, do you?" "Yes, I do, when have you known me to go out half-ass?" "I guess you're right, you always dress up, you know I was just playing with you." "You better be because Mrs. Spade isn't going out of this house unless she's got her shit together." "Ha, ha, I know that's right, do your thing Mrs. Spade, but can you do me a favor?" "What's that Bae?" "Can you please come home at a reasonable time?" "Do you mean like you did last night?" "Oh, so now, you're playing tit for tat, huh?" "No, I am not, but the last time I checked I was grown, excuse me." "You heard me, now let me say it in this tone, ha, ha, honey can you please come home at a safe time because I wouldn't want anything to happen to my beautiful wife." "Since you put it that way, I promise to get back before it's too late, now let me get out of here." "Okay, honey, I love you, have fun," I said, and I sat down to eat my breakfast and I sipped on my hot coffee, "Mmm, just like I like it," I said. Laquita ran upstairs to get dressed while I grabbed the remote to turn on the television. "I guess it will be just me and the television." Everybody deserves some me time and mines will be today.

SPADE

TWO HEARTS, TWO SOULS, ONE LIFE

A **WOMAN'S** PLACE

9

HANGING WITH THE GIRLS AT TASHA'S HOUSE

I finally made it to Tasha's house around noon. She was preparing food for all the girls. We all decided to just lounge around the house and just have some girl time. "Hey, I brought my bikini, Let's sit around the pool when you're done," I said. "That is a good idea, girl. And I just got my pool fixed." "I just love your pool, I can't wait to get in it, do you need any help with the food?" "I sure do, can you hand me those trays over there?" "Over here?" I said as I looked under her lower cabinets." "Up, up, up, higher, right, right there," Tasha said. "Okay, I got them."

At about 1:15 pm, Portia and Sabrina came over. "Hey girls," I said. "What's up, look at you looking all cute," Sabrina said. "Thank you," Tasha said. "Girl, she wasn't talking to you," Portia said. "Ha, ha. Don't you start." I said. "I am, just messing with her," Portia said.

"Portia, don't you ever stop talking?" Tasha said, "No, never, and neither do you, anyways do you need some help over there?" Portia asked. "I was just helping her," I said. "I see you have your pool fixed," Sabrina said. "It looks nice," Portia said. "Don't it, I was just telling her I brought my bikini, I am getting in that pool today," I said. "Well, you're by yourself because I didn't bring mine but I still want to get in the pool," Portia said. "How do you know I want y'all dirty asses in my pool?" Tasha said. "Dirty, dirty, girl shut up," Portia said. "I know I am not dirty," Sabrina said. "I know I'm not dirty, I smell like Bath and Body works," I said, and we all giggled.

"Y'all can't take a joke, damn, but anyhow, I have a few more girls coming by," Tasha said. "Who else?" I asked. "Linda Coleman and my cousin Tracy are supposed to be coming," Tasha said. I immediately got quiet because I can't stand Tasha's cousin Tracy, she's a homewrecker and she loves screwing married men. "Linda is cool, but why did you invite your whorish ass cousin?" Portia asked. "She's family, that's why," Tasha said. "I'm glad she isn't no kin to me," Portia said. "Y'all don't like that girl, why?" Sabrina asked, "For one, she fucks with married men," Portia said. "How do you know that, sis?" Sabrina asked. "Because that bitch tried to fuck my ex-husband and knowing them both, they fucked." Portia said. "Leave my cousin alone now, she can't help it, she was hurt by a few men and now she just doesn't care, I am not saying it's right, but it's her bed, and one day she will have to lie in it, I am just trying to help her out," Tasha said.

"Help her out, well you need to send that bitch to the psych ward or something, she's okay as long as she stays away from me," Portia said. "I know that's right," I said. "Hey, is she that bad?" Sabrina asked. Portia and I looked at Sabrina and rolled our eyes. "I guess that's bad," Sabrina said. "Can you guys please just be cordial," Tasha said. "I will think about it," Portia said, and we chuckled in devious laughter.

We kept conversing about Tracy's trifling ass until she showed up at the door. "Let me get this door, who is it?" Tasha yelled. "It's me, your cousin, Tracey, open this door girl." We all looked at each other as Tasha pointed her finger at us, as to say, "Be nice." "Here I come," Tasha said as she opened up the door. "Hey cousin, look who I drove with, look," Tracy said. "Who is that Jameson Garret, Silvia Key's husband?" Tasha whispered. "Yes, Tasha, that muthafucka buys me anything and everything," Tracy said with excitement. We tried not to listen to what she was saying but the trifling bitch was so loud. "Girl, get in here, you will reap what you sow, remember Grandma Nanna used to say that?" Tasha said. "Yeah, yeah, somebody should have told them sluts who cheated with my ex-husband years ago. "Tracy said as she walked into the house with a smug look on her face. Tracy made her a glass of wine and went and sat by the pool by herself, while we all looked at each other and just shook our heads from side to side.

"Y'all be nice, she's going through something," Tasha said. "Yeah, other women's husbands," Portia whispered and we all giggled.

Tasha got all the food done as we were talking. "I thought you said Linda was coming by?" Sabrina said. "Yeah, I haven't seen her in almost a year, what is she doing with herself?" Portia asked. "Linda is doing her, she has her beauty salon now, she's been divorced for five years, with three kids, one boy, and two girls," Tasha said. "Damn, Linda has three kids now?" I asked. "Yes, her ex-husband tried to keep her barefoot and pregnant," Tasha said. Just as we were talking the doorbell rang. "Let me get it," Tasha said.

Tracy took a sip of her drink and got up from the pool and came back into the house. "Who is it?" Tasha said. "Girl, hey, it's me, it's me, Linda." She said. Tracy took another sip of her wine and sat right next to me. I moved over slightly to the far left of her. I didn't feel comfortable with her sitting that close to me, hell, I don't trust that bitch. "Linda, hey girl, I am glad you came," Tasha said as she let her inside the house. "Hey girl, I haven't seen you guys, it seems like ages, hey girl, Laquita, come and give me a hug." I got up and gave her a big hug. "Linda, girl you haven't changed a bit, I miss you," I said. "I miss you too, we have a lot of catching up to do," Linda said with a big smile on her face. "Linda, life is truly treating you well, look at you coming in here like a boss with your Chanel bag and the shoes to match, I love that girl, I have a Louie bag and shoes that are similar," Sabrina said. "You girls and that name-brand shit," Portia said under her breath. "Oh my God, it's the twins, right, Portia and Sabrina, I miss you, girls," Linda said as she came to hug the girls. "I hear you have your own beauty salon," Portia said. "I sure do, why don't you come by and let a sister hook your hair up," Linda said. "I will take you up on that, you're right, Sabrina, this girl has stepped up her game, especially after she left that lame," Portia said. "Portia," I yelled. "It's all good, she is telling the truth, Carl was the worst man I've ever met in my life, but that is old news, water under the bridge, you know, oh hey Tracy, how are you?" Lind said. "Hi Linda, you're looking nice, oh hey, hi ladies." Tracy finally spoke to us, but we were all quiet.

"Okay ladies, all the food is done, can y'all help me take everything out near the pool," Tasha asked. We all stopped what we were doing and started helping until all the food was near the pool. "Who all have bathing suits?" Tasha asked." "I do," I said. "I do, Linda and Tracy both said. "I didn't bring one, because last I heard your pool needed work," Portia said. "That's the last I heard also," Sabrina said. "It was, but I just got it fixed, don't worry we are all about the same size, I have some new sets upstairs y'all can put on," Tasha said. "Girl, I ain't putting on nothing you had your nasty punani in," Portia said. "Portia, she said she has new sets, she just bought," I said. "Oh, okay, because I was about to say, I don't put my pussy in nothing somebody had their hot box in," Portia said and we all laughed. "You know what your problem is?" Tasha asked. "You don't listen, now come on and let's get these bathing suits on," Tasha said calmly. "I do listen, but I am ready to eat, drink, and relax, where are we going?" Portia said. "The bathing suits are upstairs in my guest closet and they are brand new, thank you," Tasha said. "Are you sure you have one to fit these wide-ass hips?" Sabrina asked, "Those aren't hips, those are wide-ass saddle bags, ha, ha." Portia said and we all laughed. "Girl hush," Sabrina said.

As Tasha and the girls went upstairs, Linda and Tracy and I poured some wine, and we headed out by the pool. We each found our chairs and just sat and stared at the water. Linda came over to talk to me, and soon after, Tracy came over also, Tracy finally started opening up and talking. I was hesitant to chat with her but I could tell something was bothering her, so I stayed cordial as I promised Tasha.

We sat there near the pool and the three of us made small talk until Tasha, Sabrina, and Portia made it back down. "Those are some pretty bathing suits," Linda said. "Yes, they are so cute," I said. "You girls are cute, let me go put mines on," Tracy said as she got up and started twitching with a nasty whorish walk. I stuck my nose up and so did Portia. We went into the bathroom & changed into our bathing suits also.

After we were all dressed, we went into the pool and we swam and played around a bit. Everyone was having a good time and surprisedly, so was Tracy. "I am getting hungry girls, let's eat and drink wine," Tasha said and we all agreed as we got out of the pool.

CHARLES LEE ROBINSON JR.

After we finished eating, Tasha poured all of us a fresh glass of wine and called us to sit at the table near the patio. "So, what do you girls want to talk about?" Tasha said. It seemed like there was a damn echo because all the women said, "Men." It seemed like a unanimous decision.

"Okay, so who's going first?" Sabrina asked. "I tell you what, let's just talk about what's going on in each of our lives that bothers us about me, how's that?" Tasha asked. "That's boring, let's talk about how all men are dogs, they ain't shit, their liars, and all they want is pussy." Tracy said. We all looked stunned because that was the most that trick said all day. "Now we are talking, I am fed up with all their lies and all the cheating," Portia said. "Girl, all men don't cheat," Sabrina said. "And, all men aren't dogs, it's just the ones I picked were, ha, ha," Linda said as she chuckled. "All men aren't bad, Brent and I get along well, not perfect but we respect each other and love each other," I said.

"Well, maybe you should stay out of this conversation," Tracy said. "Excuse me, maybe I should stay in it and give you a pointer or two," I said, and Tracy got quiet. "Oooh, "Sabrina said. "Hush, stop hyping shit up," Tasha whispered. "So, speak it, girl," Portia said. "I wasn't trying to be funny or anything Laquita, I just mean you have the perfect husband and marriage, but most of us don't," Tracy said as a form of apology. "I don't have the perfect marriage nor am I perfect or my husband, we just learned each other, he learned his position and

TWO HEARTS, TWO SOULS, ONE LIFE

I learned my place in his life, it's as simple as that, but people make it hard because they want everything now, they aren't patient and they don't give a damn about what the other person feels or been through," I said.

"That's how your life is, but mine, I have been dogged so bad, I've been humiliated, and my ex's treated me worse than a dog," Tracy said. "I know exactly what you mean, my ex-husband was a piece of work and our divorce left a nasty taste in my mouth," Portia said. "Listen before I met my husband, I had been treated badly, and my heart was broken, but I didn't let that stop me from finding love, I knew somewhere, there was love out there, and then my husband came and he changed all of that, it wasn't easy, but we did it," Sabrina said. "Well girls my husband left me broke with nothing, I didn't have a place to stay, no car., no job or anything, at one time in my life, I thought I was going to die I even thought about selling some of my goodies." Linda said as she patted her private parts "You thought about being a prostitute?" I asked. "That girl was going to sell her pussy, damn, I have to hear more of this," Portia said. "Girl, hush your mouth." Sabrina said, "Now that's deep, but look at you now, you came through." Tasha said.

"I did come through, but it was hard, and now dating these days is out the window, these guys don't have their shit together," Linda said. "That is true, and they don't know how to talk to a woman, they out here saying, hey ma, come here baby, and I'm like, who do you think you talking to, your momma, now that's what I want to say." Portia said, "I am glad I am married but I do hear this kind of talk at the hospital all day at work, even the older men talk like that and they try to act like they're still young, I just ignore them." I said.

"Yeah, when they get disrespectful, I just walk away, I am happily married and I don't have time for boys, so most of them know not to come my way with that talk," Sabrina said.

"My husband Jordan and I don't have a perfect marriage either, hell he's always out of town for work, so we make the best of our time and we make our marriage work," Tasha said. "Where is he now, Tasha?" Linda asked. "He's working at some nuclear plant in China," Tasha said. "Hell, y'all barely see each other," Tracy said. "It doesn't matter, we facetime each other on our iPhones, and when he is home we tear the whole house down," Tasha said. "Better you than me, I don't know if I could be away from my husband or man like that and still trust him," Portia said. "That's why you're you and I am me, it works for us, plus we trust each other," Tasha said. "I know that's right," I added.

"I don't trust men anymore, I've been beaten, robbed, and even stalked, that's why I don't want a man, I rather fuck with some other woman's man because I can get what I want and leave his ass right where he's at," Tracy said. "But, why mess with a married man, that's trifling, you got to do better than that, now, I am not about to mess with nobody else's husband," Linda said. "Why should I care about another woman's husband, hell they didn't care about me, when I found out all these tricks on our street slept with my ex-husband and they knew I was married, do you think they cared about making me a damn fool," Tracy screamed and then she started crying frantically.

At that moment we listened, and we understood why she was the way she was, and it made us all feel bad. We walked over to her, and we embraced her. "Listen, don't cry, we've all been through this crazy shit, but never forget your self-worth, men will only do what you allow them to, never give a man that power that he changes you into something you're not, never let them make you insecure and never do what they do, you are a lady," I said as I held her in my arms. "Tracy it will be okay cousin, we are right here for you," Tasha said. "I could tell something was on your mind," Sabrina said. "He hurt me so badly, y'all just don't know, I have lost who I am, and I just didn't give a damn anymore, he ruined me," Tracy said. "Don't let any man ruin you, I am divorced, and I'll be damn if I let a man take away my ability to heal and feel self-love, get strong and you will bounce back," Portia said. "We are all here for you," Sabrina said. Tracy cried and cried, and I must admit I felt sorry for her.

I realized at that moment that I was blessed with the marriage I have. It's not perfect but from listening to my friends talk, it could've been worse. Tracy finally stopped crying and we talked some more then I realized it was getting late and I promised Brent that I wouldn't stay out too late. "Listen, girls, it's getting late and I have to get ready to go home, hey Tasha why didn't Kemberley come over, I just thought about that?" "Kemberley is out of town with her husband, they took a cruise to the Bahamas," Tasha said. "She sure kept that a secret, she didn't tell me," I said. "Yeah, I guess it was a last-minute thing," Tasha said. "I know she's having a good time, but she's going to hate that she misses this," Sabrina said. "I haven't seen Kemberley in ages either, how's she doing, she still looks the same?" Linda asked. "Nothing changed on that girl, she's still the same and still with the same boring ass man," Portia said. "Stop hating," Tasha said. "Hating hell, I am not hating," Portia said. "He can't be too boring he took her on a cruise to the Bahamas," Linda said.

"I wish someone would take me on a cruise." Tracy said and we all looked at each other and said, "Knaw." "You girls are something else, well it has been nice, but I need to get out of here, and Tracy, honey, get my number from Tasha, we can talk over the phone but please don't come to my house, that's out, ha," I said, and everybody laughed. "I will call you; you don't have to worry about me, I don't want your husband," Tracy said. "That's good, call but don't come over," I whispered and we all laughed again.

I gave all the girls a big hug and took a to-go plate of food and I headed home. It was hurtful for me to hear all the mess these women had been going through with men. I am so glad that I am in a good place with my husband, and I thank God for that.

TWO HEARTS, TWO SOULS, ONE LIFE

♠

SPADE

10

WE STILL HAVE ARGUMENTS & DISAGREEMENTS

On my way home from Tasha's house, I thought about all the conversations that my girls and I had, and I must admit, I felt sorry for Tracy and her whorish ass. I also realized that she had been hurt so badly and sleeping with other women's husbands is the only thing she feels can heal her broken heart.

I pray one day Miss Thang gets her act together. As I pulled up into our driveway, Brent's was nowhere in sight and I noticed the garbage can was still outside, I shook my head and I left the garbage can out there. I came in and started some laundry, got in some comfortable clothes and I pulled out a glass of wine.

I thought to myself, "How is this man going to tell me to come home at a decent time and his ass isn't even here?"

Not even twenty minutes later, I heard Brent's car drive up the driveway. I just finished putting clothes in the dryer and I put more dirty clothes in the washer. Brent walked in the door, and he had this sour look on his face. He sat down and he didn't say much.

"Where have you been?" I said. "I went for a ride since you took so long to come home." He said as he snapped at me. "Hold up, what do you mean, I came in late, this isn't any later than you usually come home when you're hanging out with your friends."

"Are you trying to do everything I do?" "Listen Mr., don't start none, won't be none," I said, and he sat on the sofa with his lips poked out. I can tell he wanted to say something but I was hoping he didn't because I wasn't in the best of moods at this point.

"I know you're not mad, you know I am, always with my girls, so if you have a problem with that then I will start having a problem with you and your friends." "Go right ahead." He said. "Mr. Spade, I can't believe you have an issue over some petty shit like this, I was caught in the moment with the girls and I even told them I had to leave earlier, and I did that just for you, just to respect my husband." "Well, I wanted to take you out to dinner, or something." "How in the hell am I supposed to know that, I can't read your mind?" "If you had brought your ass home earlier, you would have known." He said. "Wait a minute, who are you cursing at, and with that tone of voice?" "You cursed first, so I gave it right back to you." "Watch your mouth, that's all I have to say, is watch your mouth, Brent." "Laquita, you watch your mouth, don't curse at me and I won't curse at you." "I guess that's fair enough, but I still can't believe you're upset." Well, believe it."

"You know what, you need to be ashamed of yourself, but since you want to come at me sideways like you're crazy or something, why is the garbage can still in front of the house, especially when the garbage truck ran over ten hours ago, huh, explain that?"

"I was sleeping most of the day and by the time I woke up, you still weren't here so I didn't even think about bringing it in." That's no excuse, you never take out the trash or bring in the trash can, until I ask you to anyways, it's like you forget just to get under my skin." I said as I kept forcing clothes into the dryer.

"You just want to argue about anything don't you?" "I am not just arguing about anything, you started it first, I thought I was doing what you asked, and you had a problem with that," I said as I watched some clothes fall back out of the dryer.

"Stop, stop, first of all, you are putting too many damn, I mean you're putting too many clothes in the dryer. "It's your fault, you are pissing me off." "Okay, okay, maybe I did overreact a bit, but it's only because I wanted to do something special for you." "Well, Brent you should have said so, then my mind would have been set on coming home at a set time that you wanted me to." "Look, I don't want to argue with you, maybe I should've said something, do you accept my apology?" "Yes, of course, will you accept mine, even though I still came in at a decent time, ha, ha." I chuckled. "You always have to win, don't you?" "Win, win what, I am just saying." "Whatever you're just saying, let me get out here and bring in the garbage can," Brent said as he headed toward the door. "Thanks, and please," I said as I took some of the clothes out of the overfilled dryer.

Brent came back into the house with the trash can and we both looked at each other in embarrassment because of the arguing and bickering over such little things.

"Are you okay, honey?" Brent said. "Are you okay?" I replied. "Yes, it's been a while since we've been in an argument or disagreement." "Yes, it has but we are allowed to, it's okay to have differences, right?" "Yes, it is, I just don't want to go to bed with you mad at me." "I feel the same way. Bae, you know I love you and I would not do anything to hurt you." "I know that, I guess I was being a little selfish but the next time, I promise to communicate a little better." And, I promise to ask you, if you have anything planned for us especially if you asked me to come home a little early."

"Okay, after all this apologizing, can we have some make-up sex?" Brent asked. I looked at him and dropped all the clothes on the floor and I said, "I thought you'd never ask."

You know sometimes, married couples have arguments and disagreements and that is a part of being in the marriage. The two of you won't always agree, but that does not mean the marriage should be over. My marriage is not perfect by far, but my husband and I know how to not let anger get in the way of our love for one another and not let things get out of hand.

Brent and I couldn't wait to get upstairs and tear the damn clothes off each other. It was like we'd never had that spat at all, now that's love.

"I love you honey, and I didn't mean to make you upset, now come over here and let me ease your mind," Brent said as he put his hands on my hips. "Same here Bae, here touch her, she's so hot," I said as I put his hands on my kitty cat. "Damn she is hot, and she's wet." "She is wet and that's because she wants you, to make love to me, my King." "I will my Queen, I will," Brent said as we lay across the bed butt naked. Our bodies collided and our flesh became one as I could feel him all inside of me. We kissed each other after every stroke entered my soul. "I love you, Laquita." "I love you, Brent." We made love for hours and hours, over and over again.

TWO HEARTS, TWO SOULS, ONE LIFE

I don't like arguing with my husband, but I sure love make-up sex. There is nothing like it in the world.

CHARLES LEE ROBINSON JR.

♠

SPADE

11

MISTAKES TURN INTO LESSONS

The next morning, I got up early so I could take a morning jog around the neighborhood before I headed into the hospital and I noticed a black Impala down the street. Just sitting there. As I ran by it on the sidewalk, I glanced over and it seemed to be two undercover officers, at least that's what they looked like to me. It kind of made me nervous, because why would the police be parked around my house?

I went into the house and told Brent, and it caused him to have a sour look on his face. "What the hell are police out there for, are you sure they're police?" "I believe so, why don't you walk by them or I mean jog by them, you don't want them to get suspicious." "Get suspicious for what." He said anxiously/ "I will go out there when I leave the house for work." "Okay, I am going to shower and get ready to go to the hospital," I said and walked upstairs cautiously. "What in the hell, why are those police out there?" I asked myself and then a thought came across my mind, "What if they are out there because of me attacking Brent's co-worker, Danyele?" At that moment, I got worried.

I started shaking as I put my clothes on leisurely. I started thinking about my career, my house, and losing my husband because I could not control myself. I just knew the police would put me in jail, I even started crying but I had to stop myself before Brent saw me.

I wiped away the tears and got myself dressed. I told Brent I loved him, and I walked out of the house, but the black Impala was gone. I started feeling a little better. I made it to work at about 9:30 am and the first person I saw was Tasha. She was sitting in the cafeteria. I had to tell her about the black Impala parked outside of my home this morning.

"See, I told your ass, you shouldn't touch that woman, I hope they're not looking for you, oh my God." She said. "I know, I know, I feel so stupid," I said as tears rolled down my eyes. "Stop, don't do that crying shit in front of me, hell I might just start crying too, but maybe you're just overacting, if they knew you did something they would just have arrested your ass, maybe they are there for someone in the neighborhood." "Maybe you're right, maybe I am overacting," I said as I paced back and forth. "Girl, get yourself together, your ass better not operate on nobody's ass today." "I am a professional, I would never let what's going on in my life affect my career." "I am just looking out for you, but yeah, I know you are professional, and you do know your shit." "Well, let me clock in and get to work, is Kemberly here today?" "Yeah, I think she is working on the 3rd floor today, you know in the cancer dorms." Okay, I will email her. "Are you going to tell her what's going on?" "Yeah, plus, I want to know more about that cruise she and her husband took, I think it's time that Brent and I get away." "I think that's a good idea, get away before you get locked away, ha, ha," Tasha said as she giggled. "Bitch, that wasn't even funny," I said as I walked away. "What, hey, you know I was just playing, Laquita, I apologize," She said as I kept walking at full speed.

"The nerve of her joking at a serious time like this. Tasha pissed me the hell off. I clocked in and walked into my office to look at all the procedures I had to do for that day and then I emailed Kemberley. Within an hour, Kemberley called me just as I was finishing up with a patient.

"Hello, Laquita, I got your email, what's going on?" "Hey, Kemberley, are you guys busy down there in the cancer dorms?" "Girl, it's always busy down here, I know you are busy also." "All the time, I can't get a break, I am so exhausted by the end of the day." I know what you mean." "That's one reason, I emailed you, I know you and your husband took that cruise a while back and I was thinking Brent and me need a trio also, can you send me some information on a good trip to take, I want to be on the water for at least seven days, just I and my husband," "Sure, I got you, girl, I will email you the trip package that we took, It was so nice and romantic, I will most definitely do it again, "Where did you guys go?" "We went to the Bahamas, and some other islands, it was beautiful and the water is so pretty." "I know it is, not like here, with this dirty, stank water." "Ha, ha, definitely not like this, but, uhm, we were on land most of the trip, I believe we were only on the water for three days, seven days is a lot on the water." Yeah, I know but I just want to unwind." "I hear you, girl; I will email you the information at lunchtime." "Okay, Kemberley there's one more thing that I want to talk to you about."

"What's that, is anything wrong, Laquita?" "Yes and no." "What, okay, please explain," Kimberley said. "Listen, Tasha is the only one I've told this to so far." "What, what is it?" "Remember Brent's co-worker, that Danyele, bitch?" "Yes, the one you whooped her ass, and she didn't know it was you, yes, yes, I remember that shit, that was bold as hell, I don't know if I would've risked it all for a piece of dick, but you did." "Hey, that piece of dick is my husband, and she was being disrespectful." "Okay, I am sorry about that, don't get so testy, so what's happening now?" "Nothing really, but lately, I've noticed the police outside of my home in an unmarked car." "They don't know you attacked that girl, do they?" "No, I don't think so but why are they parked outside of my house every day." "Did they say anything to you?" "No. they are just sitting out there and it's making me nervous as hell." "First of all, calm down, are you sure they're police?" "I am not sure, but they sure look like police?" "Have they said anything to you?" "No, not exactly, they are just posted up out there." "If they haven't said anything, I wouldn't worry about it, they probably don't know anything, don't get yourself worked up about that shit, it's probably somebody that they're looking for, girl chillout, they don't want you, if they did, you would know." "Maybe you're right, I guess I am overreacting, well thanks for that chat, don't forget to send me the information." "I won't, my lunchtime is in a half an hour, okay Laquita, don't let this worry you, just keep living your life, the police aren't after you." "I guess you're right, let me get back to work, we will chat later." "Okay, bye." "Bye," I said as I hung up the phone.

After I got through my last procedure, I clocked out and hurried home. Soon I pulled up into my neighborhood, the black Impala was back sitting across the street from my house but this time it was a little further down the street. I drove by very slowly and I took a look into the car. Two guys were sitting in there. One guy had his head down and the other one was looking through binoculars.

They didn't pay any attention to me, and I passed by. Just as I pulled up into the driveway, I could see Brent's car driving by the black Impala and slowed up just like I did. I got out of my car and Brent pulled up into the drive. "Are they still out here." He said. "They are, I wonder what they want?" I said with a nervous tone." "I am not sure but one of the guys was looking down that way, at the other end of the street," "With some binoculars, right?" I asked. "Exactly," "I hope there isn't an escaped convict or something around here." "I think they would've told us plus it would've been on the news, I don't know, I just don't know," Brent said as he headed into the house. "Yeah, I hear you, Bae, I am, right behind you," I said as we both walked into the house.

Brent and I didn't say anything to each other for about ten minutes. For some reason, he seemed so far away. I guess you could say I was the same way. Something inside of me kept saying, "Tell him what happened with his co-worker and then another part of me was saying, "Hell no, you better not tell him shit."

After we both showered, we met back downstairs and sat in the sitting room. "Laquita, there's something that I need to tell you. "That's funny because there is something that I need to talk to you about also," I said as I took a deep breath. "This is hard for me; I feel so embarrassed." He said, "That's funny, I feel the same way, well, I wouldn't say it's funny, but I am so embarrassed." "Embarrassed, why are you embarrassed?" "I don't know how to tell you, but I may know a reason why the police are posted outside of our home." "You do, that's what I wanted to say to you, I mean, I hope they're not out there for the reason I am thinking, but what are you thinking?" He asked as he looked me up and down. I could see fear in Brent's eyes, and I didn't know why. "Bae, are you okay?" "No, no, I am not, uhm, as I said, there's something you should know." "Bae, there's something you should know, can I please tell you first what's on my mind because I am scared," I said as I walked towards the window, and I could still see the black Impala parked outside. Tears started flowing out of my eyes. "Hey honey, what's going on, tell me, did anybody hurt you?" "No, no, it's nothing like that," I said as I walked towards him.

"Then what is it?" "Let me calm my nerves for a second." "Okay, here, take your time," "Remember, when you said your co-worker was attacked a few months ago?" "Yes, Danyele, from what Miss Hampton was saying, somebody put a whooping on her." He said. "Well, there's something that I need to tell you," I said as I was interrupted by the doorbell.

"Honey, hold that thought, who is it?" Brent yelled as he walked toward the door. "Who is it," Brent said. "It's the police." A man's voice said in a deep tone. My body tensed up. Brent opened the door slowly "Yes, officers, how may I help you?" "Listen, we are looking for Pedro Vasquez, he's a neighbor of yours that lives down the street, he's been wanted for sex trafficking, have you seen him?" "No, we don't even know him all that well, I mean he just moved into the neighborhood about six months ago." "Officers, I am sorry we don't know him," I said as I walked up behind Brent. "Okay, well be careful, he's a very dangerous man." The officer said. "Excuse me, sir, was that you guys sitting out there in that black Impala?" I asked. "Yes, we are undercover for this sting operation." "I knew it was something," Brent said. Instantly a weight was lifted off my shoulder. All I could think about was, damn I almost told on myself. "We will stay out here for as long as it takes, this slime ball is going down, well thank you guys, we will find this guy." The officer said. "Should we be worried, officer?" "Yes, and no, no matter what, we will be posted out here until he's apprehended." "That does make us feel a little comfortable, okay officers, thank you for letting us know." Brent said, "Yes, thank you, if we see anything we will let you know." I said softly. "Okay thanks, talk to you later, good night." The officers said.

I watched both of them walk back to the black Impala and get in. My heart started beating at its normal pace and I felt much better. I could actually see the relief on Brent's face.

"See, honey, I knew it was probably somebody down the street that they were looking for, so what's going on, why were you upset and what do you have to tell me?" "Oh, it was nothing, I was overreacting, it's nothing, I will be okay," I said. At that point, I didn't feel a need to tell Brent anything but I must admit I felt a little bad lying to him about the situation.

"Bae, what did you have to tell me?" "Tell you, oh, nothing at all, I guess I had a bad day at the office also, it's nothing that I should worry you about." "Are you sure, before the officers showed up, you looked very unedged, are you sure there isn't anything going on?" "I am positive, everything is good, but I sure hope they find that Pedro guy," I said in relief. "Me too, he must be a bad guy." "Sex Trafficking, can you believe that?" "These days, people will do any damn thing, it's a crazy world," I said. "That is true, I think I need another hot shower after that," Brent said as he wiped his forehead. "Yes, you do, your forehead was wet with sweat while you were talking to the officers, you would've thought they were looking for you, ha, ha," I said with a giggle. "You seemed pretty nervous yourself." "I am glad they are gone, now do you mind if I get in the shower with my fine, and sexy husband?" "I thought you never ask, let's go," Brent said, and we headed upstairs to the bathroom.

As I slipped out of my clothes, I thought to myself, damn, I almost told on myself, that was close. I truly love my husband and as his Queen, I have to protect our home and our marriage, it's crazy to say, that if this situation had happened with that bitch, Danyele again, I wouldn't change a damn thing!

CHARLES LEE ROBINSON JR.

♠

SPADE

TWO HEARTS, TWO SOULS, ONE LIFE

A MAN'S POSITION

12

WE CAN'T HAVE CHILDREN

The next weekend I was back over to Steven's house to play spades. Stanley and Carlos wanted revenge, so they said. "Are you guys ready to get your asses whooped in spades again?" Carlos said. "Man, we came back and spanked y'all ass the last time," I said. "So, what are you saying?" Stanley asked. "You know exactly what Brent's saying, y'all can't beat us," Steven said. "What you mean we can't beat ya'll; we beat yall the last time," Carlos said. "Yeah, after y'all started that mess about Steven and Edward, that shit wasn't right, fellas," I said. "What do you mean?" Carlos said as he looked lost. "Yeah, what do you mean, we were just asking a question?" Stanley said with laughter as he started shuffling the cards. "Y'all knew what y'all was doing, y'all was cheating, but tonight I got my head right," Steven said. "Oh, you do, huh?" Carlos asked. "You do, well does that mean your boy Edward is coming back over tonight?" Stanley asked in laughter. "Man, fuck you, that's the only way you can win and that's to get in my head and hell no, he won't be here tonight or ever," Steven said. "Ha, ha, you scared," Stanley said. "Scared of what?" Steven asked. "You're scared of him taking another one of your chicken head ass girls," Stanley said. "Man, will you guys chill out, look let's play cards, plus, I have something I would like to get off my chest," I said, and everybody just stopped what they were doing, to listen.

"Do you guys remember the guy who was messing with Laquita and I had to kick his ass?" I asked as everyone looked puzzled. "Ha, ha, uhm, no, you didn't tell us about that one," Steven said. "I didn't?" I asked. "No, you didn't, and when in the hell was this?" Carlos asked. Stanley shuffled the cards loudly and then he said, "Yeah, when the hell was this, and spill the beans now." Stanley shouted as he slammed the cards on the table.

I finally got through the story and for a moment it left them quiet and just staring at one another while shaking their heads at me. "What, what, y'all can't tell me, y'all wouldn't have done the same," I said. "I don't know what the hell I would've done but man you can go to jail for stupid shit like that," Steven said. "Or, you could've got your ass killed," Carlos yelled. "Damn, boy, are you that damn pussy whipped?" Stanley asked. "Aren't you the brilliant lawyer, but you do crazy shit like this, and we're supposed to take advice from your crazy ass?" Carlos said. "Hey, take it easy on my partner, he just does little stupid shit sometimes, your ass could have gone to jail," Steven said once more.

"That's what I wanted to tell you guys, I thought I was caught," I said. "Caught?" Steven said. "Yes, the police were outside of my house for days, they were undercover," I said. "Did they arrest your stupid, pussy whipped ass?" Stanley asked. "No, and I almost told Laquita what I'd done, but the police came by our house and said they were looking for our neighbor, and I was this close to telling her the truth," I said. "Are you dumb, or are you stupid, never tell the truth, women can't handle the truth," Stanley said. "Brent, don't ever tell her that shit, she'll think you're crazy and out of control and you might just lose your wife," Stanley said. "Man, don't listen to them." Steven said, "Do you think I should tell her, Steven, what would you have done?" "Hell, no, are you crazy or pussy whipped?" Steven said as he laughed. "See, see, ha, ha, he's both," Carlos said. "Man let's play cards," I said.

"You just want to change the subject, for your sake, I hope the police weren't there for you, because you could lose your license, your job, your wife, and your damn picket fence," Stanley said. "I admit, I should've known better, but I know now," I said. "I bet you do, you got scared when you thought those police were about to arrest your ass, do you think Laquita knows? Carlos asked. "No, I don't, she couldn't have," I said. "You are a fool, let's play cards now," Steven said. "Yeah, let's do that," I said. "Ha, ha, you are a crazy ass fool," Carlos said. "Pussy whipped, ha, ha," Stanley said. "Fuck you, and let's play cards I said." "Y'all ready to get y'all ass kicked now, huh?" Stanley said as he shuffled the cards and then asked Steven to cut the deck. "Y'all are about to get it now," Carlos yelled, and we started playing our game of spades.

Steven and I were winning two games to one and Stanley started asking questions about Laquita and me again. "Man, y'all are kicking our ass, let me go get some more liquor, I am going to the store, and I will be right back," Carlos said. "Man, Carlos, I swear, you are a damn alcoholic," Steven said. "No, I am not, I just like to drink, fool," Carlos said as he got up and walked out of the door.

"Brent, I just have to ask you, have there been any other differences that you and Laquita been through, I mean have you and her ever been so mad at each other that y'all didn't want anything to do with each other?" Stanley asked. "Of course, they have fool, no relationship or marriage is perfect," Steven said. "Of course, Stanley," I said. "No one is talking to your ugly boy, why don't you go get a facelift or something, I mean I am tired of looking at that ugly face," Stanley said. "Who are you talking to with your lame ass, this is my house, you can get the hell out if you don't like my face," Steven said. "Oh yeah, you're right, ugly, I mean Brent, can you please answer my question," Stanley said as he directed his insult from Steven to me.

"Yes, in fact, Laquita and I got into it because we can't have children," I said. "Why would she get mad about that?" Stanley asked. "Damn, this is going to be interesting, because I always wondered why you two didn't have any children," Steven said. "I shouldn't be telling y'all my wife and I business, but hey, I know I can trust you guys, but anyways, Laquita thought it was my fault that we couldn't have children," I said. "Your fault, how?" Stanley said. "Let me tell y'all the story, but the short version," I said. "So, she thought it was your fault, well, was it?" Steven asked. "Man, let him tell the story," Stanley said. "Yes, please," I said as I began to tell them what happened.

IN THE PAST:

"Bae, listen, we are well set in our careers, I think it's time that we expand our family," Laquita said. "Are you sure that's what you want, I mean it is true that we are set, but are we ready to raise a family?" I asked. "Brent, yes, God, yes, it's time, don't you want to have children?" I mean yes, whatever you want baby, yes, let's get started." "You nasty boy, let's get it started, tonight." She said. "Tonight, well tonight it is."

Laquita and I tried to have children, but every month, her period came on. We tried for a whole year, and finally, Laquita started getting very inquisitive.

TWO HEARTS, TWO SOULS, ONE LIFE

"Brent, is there something wrong with you, why can't you get me pregnant?" "What do you mean, why can't I get you pregnant, maybe it's you and not me." "I don't see how it's me, my period comes every month, so you need to go to the doctor and get Mr. Willie checked out." She said with an attitude.

"Well, if I have to see a doctor or a specialist, so should you, don't try to put it all on me," I said. "I can't believe there is anything wrong with me." "How do you know?" "Because I am a doctor." "That doesn't mean shit." "Brent, don't you curse at me, now, did I curse at you?" "I am not cursing at you, I am just saying." "If I don't curse at you, then you damn sure won't curse at me." "So, now you're getting an attitude about anything." "No, I am not, I am just frustrated, we've been trying for a while now, and still nothing, I want children from my husband." "I know you do, and I want children also, so, let both of us plan to go see a specialist and see what the problem is," I said as I inhaled. "Okay, we both can make the appointment on the same day," Laquita said as she exhaled.

"Brent, what happened after that?" Stanley asked. "I am back." Carlos said as he opened the door and slammed it behind him." "Man, don't slam my door like that, or you can get your ass out of my house," Steven said. "Man, I am sorry that was a mistake, damn, now what did I miss?" Carlos asked. "I was just about to finish my story," I said. "Go ahead, Brent, these fools need to be ignored," Stanley said. "Man, this is my house," Steven said. "Shut up, yeah, I said it, in your house, now in your face, now what's up partner?" Carlos said with a smile on his face. "Can I finish my story, you two can kiss later." "Ha, ha, kiss and make up," Stanley said. "I ain't kissing Mr. Ugly over here," Carlos said. "I damn sure ain't going to kiss Mr. Lame Ass," Steven said.

"Are you two, going to listen, or what?" I said as I interrupted Carlos and Steven's bickering. Stanley just kept laughing. "Stanley, don't you laugh at these two, now, ha, ha, let me finish," I said as I couldn't help laughing at Carlos and Steven talking shit to each other as if they were a loving couple, it was hilarious.

"I walked out of the doctor's office with a blank look on my face. I was about to head towards the elevator and Dr. Givens called me back into his office."

IN THE PAST:

"Mr. Spade, I called you back in here because I want to make things clear, just because you have a very low sperm count doesn't mean that you can't ever have children, you and your wife can talk about adopting." He said. "But doc, it's not the same, my wife wants children, what am I to tell her, look, honey, my sperm count is too low, and I can't have children?" "This is not the end of the world, you are not alone, there are a lot of men in your position, if your wife truly loves you, you two can talk and work this out." He said. "I guess you're right." "But, in the meantime, I would like for you to come

back in a few weeks, so we can run a few more tests to make sure." "Man, I don't know what I am going to tell my wife." "Try to tell her the truth, and get some counseling, that may help the both of you, I am sorry, but that's all the advice that I can give today." "Okay, thank you, doctor," I said as I walked out of his office with my head down. "Mr. Spade, don't forget to go to the front desk and schedule your next appointment three weeks from today." He said. "Okay, I will," I said as I walked out of the office with tears running down my cheeks.

"Damn, I am sorry to hear that, Brent," Steven said. "A low sperm count, boy your dick is weak like that?" Stanley said with laughter. "Man, have some compassion for this weak dick son of a bitch," Carlos said. "Y'all stupid, it's not funny that this man can't have any kids, that shit is devastating," Steven said. "Thanks, Steven, I should've kept my business to myself," I said. "No, man, come on now, I am just playing with you, I know that's a hard pill to swallow," Stanley said with a serious look on his face. "Besides the jokes, man, I apologize, I know that must have been tough," Carlos said. "Yes, it was and it still is," I said. "Brent, what happened then and how did Laquita take it?" Steven asked. "Now this is the crazy part, now check this shit out," I said as they stood still while listening to me tell the rest of my story. "After my appointment, I went home, and Laquita was sitting on the sofa crying. I didn't know why so I tried to find out but she just kept crying. I knew right then, that wasn't the best time to tell her that I couldn't have children." I said.

CHARLES LEE ROBINSON JR.

IN THE PAST:

"Honey, what's wrong, why are you crying, and what did the doctor say at your appointment?" I asked as tears started flowing. "Honey, stop crying please, and tell me what has got you so upset," I said. "Brent, I have to tell you, I didn't get any good news today." She said.

"What do you mean you didn't get any good news?" "Come close to me, I am so embarrassed." "Embarrassed about what?" "I have some bad news, the doctor said they found a small mass on my uterus and that's one reason I haven't been able to conceive kids." "A mass, now what does that mean, what's a mass?" "It's you know, cancerous," she said as she started crying while putting her head down in the palm of her hands.

"Cancer, oh no honey, this sounds serious, "It can be if I don't have the surgery right away." "Surgery, no, no, is that what the doctor said?" I said with tears running down my face. "That is what they said, so I apologize for blaming you for not being able to have children. "There's no need to apologize, this is serious and all I care about is your health." "Thank you, Bae, I truly need your support right now, thank you for being by my side." "I will always be by your side, but honey, you are not alone in this, the doctors also gave me bad news today also, but now that I hear yours, it's not as nearly as bad." "What, now I know you're going to leave me because I can't have any children." She yelled out. "What, leave you, what are you talking about, I am not ever going to leave you, as I said I got some bad news too, my doctor said I can't have any kids also."

"What, why, what's the problem?" she asked as she started panting. "He said I have a very low sperm count, he said it's the lowest he's ever seen." "You can't have children either, no this can't be, neither one of us, Bae, what are we going to do?" "What are we going to do, that's a silly question, we are going to keep loving each other and staying by each other side, Laquita, I love you."

"Brent, I love you too, with all my heart." "Now, what are we going to do about this cancer?" "Doctor said I needed to schedule surgery soon as possible." "Then let's pray and hope for the best, no matter what, I am never leaving your side. "That's so sweet, but what are we going to do about having children?" "Maybe look into adopting or something down the line, but first we must worry about your health." "Mr. Brent Spade, you know what?" "What, Mrs. Spade?" "I love you." She said as she kiss me gently.

"Damn, so neither one of you can have children and y'all still stayed together, now that's love," Stanley said. "Yes, that's touching, so do you think you guys will ever adopt?" Carlos asked. "Probably one day," I said. "Well, it's a good thing you both can't have children," Steven said. "And, why is that?" I asked. "Because, it seemed like she was going to get rid of your low sperm-counting ass, ha, ha," Steven said in laughter. "Man, fuck you," I said. "He is right though," Stanley said. "Ha, ha, ha, ha." Carlos laughed as he pointed his finger at me. "You all can go straight to hell," I said as a smirk crossed my face.

A thought came across my mind as I was leaving Steven's house that night, what if it were only me who had the problem having children, would Laquita have left me?

♠

SPADE

13

PLANNING A CRUISE

{PRESENT TIME}

I walked into my office that Monday morning while trying to make it to my desk before I ran into Miss Hampton. That woman loves to gossip about everybody and everything and sure enough soon as I went to close my office door, she put her foot in the door.

"Hold up Mr. Spade, I have something to tell you, by the way, how are you and your wife doing, you don't talk about her much, but anyways did you hear about Mr. Lynell and Sonya Quest, they have been sleeping with each other and both of their spouses found out." "What, no, I haven't heard, and Laquita and me, are doing just fine, so if you don't mind Miss Hampton, I have some work to do," I said as I respectfully showed her to the door. "Did I tell you I saw Miss Danyele at the grocery store, and she didn't even speak to me, the nerve of her, okay Mr. Spade, I get the hint, you have work to do, but I will be back later, I have something juicy to tell you." "Miss Hampton, please don't come back today, I will be busy today with clients." "I will talk to you later," She said as she acted as if she hadn't heard anything I said. My morning was already starting wrong but that all changed once I received a phone call from Laquita.

"Hey, Bae, I want to talk to you about something." "Hey my love, what's wrong?" "Oh, nothing, I've been talking to my friend Kemberley, she and her husband went on a cruise a few months back and I want us to go on a short one." "Wow, that sounds good, where and when?" "Just like that, Bae, for real, can we go on one?" "Of course, we can, hell I do need time away from the office and work, what's your schedule look like?" "I can take off anytime I want, I have the time in." "Okay, where are we going?" "I am not sure, that's what I'm working on." "It has to be somewhere hot and warm, and with beautiful palm trees, and torques colored water." "I do agree, maybe, Jamaica, San Juan, or the Dominican Republic, let me look into prices and things and I will get back to you around noonish." "Okay, honey, just let me know." "I will, I am, so ready for this Baecation." "Ha, ha, what, a Baecation huh, yeah we both need that." "That's right, a much-needed vacation with my Bae." "Ha, ha, I got you, honey, I will talk to you later," I said as I hung up the phone.

Soon as I hung up the phone, I looked up, and that damn Miss Hampton was at my door again. "Miss Hampton, don't you have work to do?" "Yes, I do smarty pants, but I just wanted to tell you something." "Tell me what, I have work to do." "I just wanted to tell you that I overheard the higher-ups talking about Miss Danyele might be coming back to work in the office." "What, that's crazy, that can't be, anyways, I am not worried about her, I have a cruise coming up with my wife." "A cruise, wow, that's exciting, where are you guys going?" "Laquita said she doesn't know yet, but we were talking about Jamaica, San Juan, or the Dominican Republic." "No, don't go there, go to the Bahamas or the Virgin Islands, I don't like Jamaica, much, unless you going to Montego Bay, San Juan, isn't fun and D.R., it can be boring, and don't you remember a couple went missing there?" Miss Hampton said she kept rambling at the mouth.

"Look, Miss Hampton, this is me and my wife's trip, we don't need your input, now if you can, please exit my office I have work to do." "That's rude, but don't you want to know what happened to Evan and Mr. Randolph?" "Who, no, no, no, go, go, out, Miss Hampton "But." "Goodbye," I said as I nudged her out of my office, and locked the door behind me.

An hour later, Laquita called me and said she wanted to go on the cruise that was going to Jamaica and I laughed. "Brent, what is so funny?" "Miss Hampton was just in my office, and she was saying going to Jamaica wasn't a good idea." "How in the hell does she know where we are going?" "I accidentally told her because she keeps coming in my office gossiping about every damn body and every damn thing," I said as I inhaled with a deep breath. "Brent, stop telling that woman our damn business, and besides no one cares what she thinks." "I know you're right; I shouldn't have told her anything." "That woman talks too damn much, don't make me come to your office and tell her ass off." "Honey, please don't, I will handle Miss Hampton, so Jamaica it is." "Yes, and a few other islands." "Sounds good, we will talk more about it tonight, how's everything at the hospital?" "The same, it's overwhelming, but I am handling it." "You're a strong woman, you can handle anything." Thank you, Bae, but sometimes, I don't know about that." "You are, believe me, I am your husband, if anybody should know, I do." "You're so sweet, how did I end up with such a loving husband like you?" "You just got lucky, ha, ha." "Ha, ha, is that was it was? Luck, huh?" "Ha, ha, we both were lucky, okay, talk to you later, honey." "Bye, Bae, back to work," Laquita said with a sigh.

I managed to stay away from Miss Hampton for the rest of the day. I was lucky enough to get out of the office early due to a couple of rescheduling issues. That evening Laquita and I made all our plans to take our cruise. We were both excited because it was much needed. I just couldn't wait.

CHARLES LEE ROBINSON JR.

SPADE

14

THE BAECATION

The day came for our cruise. Laquita and I drove to the airport, and we parked our car in the airport's parking lot. "Honey, do you have everything?" "Of course, I do." "Are you sure, because this bag is heavy as hell?" "Ha, ha, well you know a woman has to pack enough." "What's enough? Damn, you have enough stuff in here as if we're going to stay a month, it's one short cruise. "A woman never knows what she needs, so I packed more than enough." "Well, I see that." "Brent, stop, talking about me, and let's catch this plane to Miami before we miss the flight." "We better not miss this flight," I said as I struggled to carry her heavy ass bag.

We finally made it on the plane, and it was packed. I was so happy because Laquita happened to get us some good seats in front of the plane. I got my favorite seat near the window and Laquita sat in the middle next to a woman who was just a little too big for that seat. As she sat down, Laquita looked over at me and gave me a sour look. "Damn, can they make these seats a little bit bigger?" She whispered. I smiled, closed my eyes, and I laughed as we got ready for takeoff.

CHARLES LEE ROBINSON JR.

The plane landed in Miami right on time and we caught an Uber to the cruise ships docking. I still struggled with Laquita's heavy ass bag, and she just laughed at me. "Don't worry I will get you back for this." "Ha, ha, Bae, what did I do?" "Ha, ha, you know this bag was too damn heavy." "Ah, man, aren't you the man, grrr?" she said as she growled while making muscles with her little arms. "Ha, ha, funny," I said as we got on the ship.

Laquita and I settled in our cabin and I immediately jumped on the bed. I was tired as hell from carrying our luggage. "Are you tired Bae?" "Ha, ha, ha, you are so funny," I said as I laid my head back on the soft pillows. I must have fallen asleep because I was awakened by the loud horn. "Did, we leave the dock yet?" I asked as Laquita was putting our clothes up. "Yes, you did, but it was a short nap."

"I guess I was tired, come here honey, come give me a big kiss and a hug." "Okay, let me hang these shirts up." Hurry, hurry, I need you." "You need me, huh, is that right?" "Stop playing and come here." Laquita walked over to the bed and I pulled her close. "You know, I needed this vacation, honey," I said. "So did I, so, did I." We lay there in bed all cuddled up. It felt so good to be with my wife and out on the water. It was so romantic and exclusive. These are the little things that keep couples together. Doing things with the one you love is priceless. "Bae, we have to get up." She said. "Why?" "It's time for dinner." "Damn, already, Mr. Willie and I were thinking about having you for dinner." "Ha, ha, well my stomach is talking and from the sound of things, so is yours, now get up so we can get dressed and go get something to eat, and then we can get freaky later tonight." "Okay, I like the sound of that, let me get up now." "Ha, ha, that's all it takes to get you up huh, do you see this kitty?" Laquita said as she patted her private parts. A huge smile came across my face. I got up and we both took a shower together, got dressed and we headed out for dinner.

After a romantic dinner, we went for a walk on the ship. The water was so calming, and the moon was shining brightly. "Isn't it beautiful, Bae?" "Yes, it is, we should've done this a long time ago," I said as we kept walking. We walked all around the ship and then we met a few married couples who were also on vacation on the ship. Thomas and Mary have been married for fifteen years and they were from Seattle, Washington, and Shane and Melonie were from Atlanta, Georgia and they were married for twenty-five years.

They talked Laquita and me into going to the pool and the jacuzzi, so we went back to our cabin and put on our clothes to get in the pool, and grabbed our towels. "Damn you look good honey, and look at all that sexiness." "You know I am not going out there like this, I need to put on my wrap." "Why honey, you look good." "Well, thank you, but all of this is for you, not for the world to see." "Okay, then, put on your wrap since you put it that way," I said as I gently grabbed her ass. Laquita giggled and she got her wrap and then put it on. "Now, are you ready?" "Yes, I am, let's go get in the pool, Bae." "I am with you."

CHARLES LEE ROBINSON JR.

We went out and we had a wonderful time, talking and having drinks with our new friends. It was getting late and the guys wanted to hang out later, but I wanted to stay with my beautiful wife, Laquita. "Brent, the ladies want to hang out, but I want to spend this time with you." "Yeah, and so do the guys, but I want to be with you, so let's go back to the cabin, and let's create some magic." "I am with you, come on big daddy." "Ha, ha, big daddy, huh, let's go," I said.

We said our good nights to our new friends and we held hands until we reached our cabin. Once we got back, we immediately jumped into the shower and then got ready for bed. "I love you honey, and I am so glad you set up this cruise." I love you too, Bae, it was much needed and I know the both of us need this." "We have been through so much and we still managed to keep things together." I said, "Yes, we have, neither one of us, know it hasn't been easy, and what we have is special." "I agree, that's why I would never let you go, you are my heart and no matter what we go through, I will always pray to God that he makes our journey together an easy one." "I pray that all the time, Bae, you are my heart, and it took us a long time to get to this place, but I am here for the long haul," Laquita said.

One thing I love about my wife and I relationship and marriage is the respect we have for one another and that helps us whenever we face hard times. We conversed a little longer and then became intimate with our hands and then our bodies followed. We made love for hours, both mentally and physically and that's the best kind of love-making a husband and wife can have.

The next morning, the ship docked in Montego Bay, Jamaica. We got off the ship for a few hours. We enjoyed the food and the good drinks and then we were right back on the ship just relaxing. "I have enjoyed this trip, with just you and I," Laquita said. "Me too, but we will be back to reality in a day." "I know, let's make these memories last a lifetime." "We are already doing that," I said.

After a couple more stops and getting off the cruise ship, we were heading back toward Miami. This trip did wonders for both of us. We opened up to each other about our feelings. And we enjoyed every moment of just cuddling and kissing. One thing I learned from being with Laquita for these few days is that I don't want to live without her. She's the one that makes my heart beat and I am hers, and it's sad to see that most marriages aren't as strong as ours these days. All it takes is time, patience, and understanding, and a woman's place and a man's position will form naturally. As they say, "Teamwork makes the dream work, and that couldn't be any truer.

CHARLES LEE ROBINSON JR.

♠

SPADE

TWO HEARTS, TWO SOULS, ONE LIFE

A **WOMAN'S** PLACE

15

FINANCIAL STRESS

After our trip, me and the girls met over at Kimberley's house. Her husband was out of town, so we thought it would be the right place for us to meet up. "Hey, girls, what's up?" Kemberley said. "Hey, Kemberley," I said. "Hi girls come on in, hey, Portia, Sabrina, Tasha, come on in." "Where is your husband, I heard he was out of town?" Portia asked. "Damn, that's none of our business," Tasha said. "He's in New York City for his job, so that is correct, he is out of town, now, y'all make yourselves comfortable." Kemberley said, "I am not talking to you," Portia said as she rolled her eyes. "Can you girls be nice to each other for once in your lives?" I asked. "I know, they always saying some shit stuff to one another," Sabrina said. "No, we don't." Tasha and Portia shouted. "Well, okay, then," Sabrina said.

"Don't y'all want to know about my cruise, it was so nice, thank you Kemberley for helping me set that up, Brent just loved it," I said. "You are welcomed, I knew you would," Kimberley said. "Next time, let's do a couple's cruise with all our husbands," Tasha said. "I don't have a husband." Portia said." Then your lonely ass won't be coming."

Tasha said. "We were all stunned from hearing that comment. "Bitch, I am not lonely, and I can still go," Portia yelled. "Ladies, ladies, please keep it down, I do have neighbors, you know?" Kemberley said. "Stop all this unnecessary bickering and let me tell you about my cruise." I said, "Yes, I have to hear this because my husband and I will be included on the next couple's cruise," Sabrina said, Then, I smiled and I winked my eye at her. "Well, I guess I will be the third wheel because I damn sure won't be remarried by then," Portia said and we all laughed. "It's okay Portia, you will still have fun and you might meet your future husband on the cruise," Kemberley said. "I doubt that shit." Tasha whispered in my ear." "Hush," I said. "What did you say?" Portia asked. "I wasn't talking to you," Tasha said as she rolled her eyes at Portia. "Will y'all stop it, please?" Sabrina said.

After Portia and Tasha stopped talking about each other, I told the girls about my cruise. "It was one of the best times I've had in a long, long time," I said. "It sounded like you guys had a good time, I will be on the next trip," Tasha said. "Yes, it sounds like fun, you can count me in also," Sabrina said. "Yes, my husband and I enjoyed that cruise too, when we went." Kemberley added, "So can I ask you a question?" Portia said. "Oh boy, here we go?" Sabrina said. "Yup, here we go?" Tasha whispered to herself and started shaking her head. "Y'all don't even know what I am about to ask her," Porta said. "Go ahead and ask," I said. I knew it was going to be something cynical. "Who paid for the cruise?" Portia asked and we all looked at her as if she was confused. "Who paid for the trip, does that even matter?" Tasha said. "This girl is crazy," Sabrina said. "They are married, does it matter who paid?" Kemberley said. "I am asking her, not y'all," Portia said as she looked me directly in the eyes. "If you must know, Kemberley help me set up the cruise but Brent and I, we both paid for everything, right down the middle, why?" I asked. "I was just curious that's all, it would've been nice if he paid it all, men are always supposed to pay," Portia said. "I don't know who in the hell told you that, but that is wrong, if you're married to someone, it's always good that you share everything and I would go as far as to say split everything down the middle," I said. "That's why your husband divorced your ass, you think he's supposed to pay for everything, something is wrong with you," Tasha said. "For your information, I divorced him," Portia said.

"You need to stop that way of thinking twin," Sabrina said. "You'll never keep a man that way," Kemberley added. "A woman should never pay for anything, that's what I think," Portia said. "This will be one lonely hoe," Tasha said. "You are the hoe, and your husband is pimping you," Portia said. "Ladies, ladies, stop it, hey I must admit, I used to think just like Portia, but in time, I grew out of that and that's one reason, Brent and I are still together," I said. "You did?" Portia asked. "And, what happened that made you change your mind?" Sabrina asked. "I have never believed in being like that, me and my husband share," Tasha said. "That's you, so what happened, and what made you change your mind?" Portia asked again. "Okay this is how I was, and believe me, now that I look back at it, it wasn't pretty, and keeping a closed mind like that, could've led me to be alone and not with the good husband that I have now, you can say I grew up, in time, we all do, or at least we should, now check this out."

IN THE PAST:

"Brent, I am paying all these bills and for three years you still haven't been able to fit the bill on your half of things." "I am trying, right now they only have me as an intern, and I am working side jobs just so I can help out when I can." "I am not here to pay for a grown man, I understand that you're trying but right now trying isn't paying the bills, I am." "All you think about is bills, I understand that things must get paid but you're supposed to be encouraging me, not tearing me down." "I am not tearing you down, but you are the man, and you are supposed to be the head of the household, that means all the bills lie on you, I am not supposed to pay anything." "Who in the hell told you that?" "That's what I was taught, a woman's place is to take care of the household while you, the man pay all the bills."

"I don't mean to burst your little bubble, but that's the old way, women have fought for equal rights, so that means, we should split things down the middle." "Well, Mr. Smart Ass, where's your half?" "It's coming soon, you watch, I will be a big-time lawyer, and one day you might need me, so I am asking you as my wife to please be patient." "I am patient, and I have been patient for a while." "Do you love me, Laquita?" "Of course, I do, but love doesn't pay any bills."

"Okay, now, I am warning you, so don't be that way, one day the money will run out, but true love will still be here." "Women should not have to pay bills, but I will be patient, only because I love you, but you have six months and then we may have to get out of this lease and go our separate ways." "Are you threatening me, because there are other women, who would love to have a chance with me?" "And, there are other men who would love to have a chance with me, so, let's not take it there," I said with anger. "Keep being that way, one day, the tides will turn and you will need me," Brent said as he stormed out of the house.

"Brent and I argued all the damn time when it came to money." "Damn, he threatened you about other women wanting to be with him?" Portia said. "Yes, he did and I threatened his ass back," I said. "That would've pissed me off too," Sabrina said. "Men, think we are the bank all the time, hell I don't need a man's money, because I got my own but still, you must pay your way when you're dealing with me, my husband knows better," Tasha said. "Yeah, that was back then, Brent and I have an understanding now, hell, I even have a bank account with him and I also have one by myself, that he knows nothing about," I said. "I know that's right, just in case his ass gets froggy and wants to leap into someone's panties, ha, ha," Sabrina said and we gave each other high-fives.

"So, finish telling us what happened because you two worked things out because you guys are still together, many years later, and going strong," Portia said.

"Six months, Brent got hired at the Lawyer firm he's in now, and things were starting to get better between us until I was let go at Genesee Hospital," I said. "Why, did they let you go?" Sabrina asked. "You know they shut down that hospital," Tasha added. "Exactly, they were getting rid of all their top-paying doctors, and I happened to be one of them," I said. "I see, so, now hubby had to take care of you, how did he take that?" Portia asked.

"At first, I was embarrassed and I was afraid to tell Brent because of all the heat that I put on his ass in the past about having your own money and paying your way," I said. "I bet his ass was gloating and everything when you told him," Sabrina said. "He probably wanted to dump your ass, and get one of those other women that he was talking about," Portia said.

"Nope, when I finally got the nerve to tell him, Brent was nothing but supportive, he picked my spirits up and he paid all the bills without question, and it made me feel like an ass," I said. "If he was an asshole, he could've treated you as you treated him in the past," Tasha added. "Now, that's a real man," Sabrina said. "Exactly, because any other man would've left your broke ass out in the cold and on the corner with a sign that says, I will work for food, ha, ha," Tasha said with laughter. "That's right, but Brent helped me change my attitude when it comes to money, he stepped up, and when I finally got the job at Highland hospital, we got back on track," I said. "You picked the right man, and it's obvious he picked the right woman, because, I would've let his ass go with those other women," Portia said. "If I would have, I would be alone and not with the good man that I have today, relationships are more than the value of money, never let money be the reason that the two of you are together because the relationship or marriage won't go far, and that's what my husband taught me," I said. "Well, I am still trying to get that point, but I get it, I understand," Tasha said. "I do too, it's about sharing and having each other's back no matter what," Sabrina said. "I guess, I will get there one day, but for now, they are paying for everything, ha, ha," Portia said. "Your dumb ass hasn't learned anything from what Laquita's telling you, yup, bitch, you will definitely be alone," Tasha said to Portia.

"I am not alone, I won't always be alone, and if you know what's good for you, you'll leave my ass alone, okay?" Portia said to Tasha. "Whatever, you are all bark and no bite, I ain't worried about you," Tasha said. "Girls, chill out, do I always have to be y'all referee?" I said. "It's obvious, you do," Sabrina said. "I am going to leave you girls with this message, there isn't a perfect marriage or relationship, they both take time and patience, respect, honesty, and loyalty, it takes a lot of shit, so be willing to put your all in but also know that your partner is willing to do the same, and never let money, be the reason that you're in a marriage or relationship, because sooner or later that house will start crumbling down," I said.

I guess that talk with the girl resonated. They all got quiet and I could see they were thinking about what I said. Sometimes, it's good to take advice from a person who has gone through it all. Brent and I put so much time in and we also learned from our mistakes.

CHARLES LEE ROBINSON JR.

♠

SPADE

16

PROTECTING OUR VOWS

After the cruise, I took a few days off before I went back to the office, but when I got there, it felt like I'd never left. As soon as I made it to my office, Miss Hampton was waiting for me. It pissed me off because all I wanted to do was come to work.

She started gossiping about every damn thing, she even started talking about how much she hated being a lawyer. "Miss Hampton, I don't have any time for this. I just got back from my trip." "Well, what do you have time for?" Miss Hampton said as she winked her eye. That shit caught me off guard and I said, "Excuse me, did you wink your eye at me?" "Stop playing, Mr. Spade, you know I have had my eyes on you for a while now, why do you think I make an excuse to talk to you about all this juicy drama at this job?" "You do know I am married, right?" "Yes, I know that and I also know that you're a fine, smart, and sexy lawyer, but no one has to know." "No one has to know what?" "How I really feel about you." "Yes, they do." "Who?" "My wife, so stop with your advances now, please." "Mr. Spade, you know I just like having fun, I wasn't serious, I was just playing with you."

"Okay, well, then play yourself outside of my office, thank you, Miss Hampton," I said, and she left quickly—the nerve of that woman to disrespect me and my wife like that.

That evening, I went home to tell Laquita about my day, but as soon as I got into the house, she was yelling and cursing about what had happened at her job. "What's wrong, honey? I can see something is bothering you." "Yes, it is, every day there's always some little asshole trying to talk to me, and today, one of the guys kept trying to talk to me, and I told him repeatedly, that I am not interested, then he had the nerve to call me an old stuck up, bitch." "Say what, he called you what, did you go to human resources?" "No, I didn't but I plan on doing it if he approaches me like that again." "Honey, why wait?" "I just don't want this to interfere with my job, a lot of these young guys are rude and don't know how to talk to a woman."

"I don't like this one bit. Is he a doctor?" "No, he works in the operating rooms as a cleaner or something." "And he thinks it's okay to disrespect you like that?" "Bae, this generation of men is all disrespectful." "What is this man's name?" "They call him Ray, Ray, but his real name is Larry." "If he keeps fucking with you, let me know, and I will pay him a visit." "Brent, please don't, I will take care of it." "Okay, you better, I am not playing, I am your husband, I am your protector, and that's what I am here to do, protect you." "I know, I know, it's just I don't want you to go to jail or get into any trouble about some young punk." "Believe me, I know how to handle things; it won't go that far." "Brent, just, don't." "Okay, handle it then." Laquita agreed to handle it, and I was so upset that I forgot to discuss Miss Hampton's advances with her.

The next day was more of the same. Miss Hampton was waiting near my office. When I walked up this time, she was eating a banana, and she intentionally rolled it and started sucking on it in front of me. I had to grab her arm and I pushed her into my office and I said, "Miss Hampton, stop doing that shit before you get me and you fired, now I mean it." "What, what did I do? I was only eating my banana?" "I am not playing with you, stop these advances." "You know you want some of this good coochie." "What, Miss Hampton get your horny ass out of my office now," I said as I slammed the door behind her.

I couldn't even work the rest of the day. I left and went home around noon. I was trying to figure out my next move. Miss Hampton sexually harassed me, and I knew I could not let it go on any longer.

I waited for Laquita to get home that evening. When she got there, she was irate. "What happened, did that punk fuck with you again today?" "Yes, he did with his vulgar mouth, I went to H.R. but she was on vacation, so I left her a message to contact, me when she gets in." "There has to be someone else that you can report that to." "I also told my higher-ups, and they said they will talk to him." "This is crazy, we are both going through crazy shit at our jobs." "We are, you didn't tell me you were having problems at your job, is it clients or something?"

"No, it's not the clients, actually, it's Miss Hampton's old, cougar ass, she keeps coming on to me." "She keeps what, you didn't tell me this, how long has this been going on?" "Soon as we returned from the cruise, she's been acting strange." "No, you mean that bitch is horny, so what are you going to do about it?" "I am going to let my colleagues know if it continues." "No, you're not waiting that long, just like you told me, if you don't get her straight, I will, and I mean it, Brent," Laquita said as she grabbed her car keys and she headed for the door.

"Where are you going?" I asked. "I am going to get a few things from the grocery store so we can have dinner tonight." "Oh, I thought we had something to eat." "No, I changed my mind about cooking that." "Okay, I guess, I will go by Steven's house for an hour or so." "Okay, don't be gone too long, dinner will be waiting, and I don't want it to be cold about time you make it back." "Okay, honey, I will make it quick." "And, so will I." She said as she hurried out the door and jumped into her car. I could see Laquita speeding down the street when the speed limit sign clearly said thirty-five miles an hour, it looked like she was doing fifty miles an hour.

As soon as she was out of sight, I jumped into my car and headed to Laquita's job. It was a must that I talk with this young, disrespectful ass young man. No one will disrespect my wife like that, and if I don't step up as her husband to protect her, then who will?

TWO HEARTS, TWO SOULS, ONE LIFE

I walked through the hospital and I stopped a few people I knew, I asked them who was this Larry guy, and finally, someone I knew pointed his ass out. I walked over to him kindly and said, "Listen, I am Laquita Spade's husband. Can I talk to you for a second?"

"Hey man, what is this about?" he asked nervously. "You know what the hell it's about," I said in a whisper as I pulled him close. "Look, Mr. Spade, is it? I don't want any problems." "If that's true, you won't say anything else to my wife, do I make myself clear?" "Yes, sir, I am sorry, sir, I was just playing with her." "Don't play with my wife, ever, do you hear me?" "Yes, I hear you loud and clear." He said as I could see the fear on his face.

On my way out I pointed my finger at him and said, don't fuck with my wife, or else I will be back, boy." I said as I calmly walked away. I drove back home, and I made it just in time for dinner. "You weren't gone that long, are you sure you went to Steven's house?" "Yes, I did, I told you, I wouldn't be that long," "Yes, you did, come on, now, dinner is ready," Laquita said. I ate, showered, and went to bed. The next day, I went to work, expecting to see Miss Hampton, but she wasn't there. Finally, I saw her walking in the hallway and she didn't even look my way. I was shocked because she usually had something to say. From that day on, Miss Hampton and I only spoke about work. I don't know what happened to change her mind, but I was happy she stopped coming on to me.

CHARLES LEE ROBINSON JR.

SPADE

17

SPIRITUAL GROWTH

"Bae, it's Saturday morning, why are you getting up so early?" Laquita asked. "You know I have to take the trash out this morning." "Oh, right, you remembered without me telling you, somebody is paying attention." "Ha, ha, let me get up." "Okay, Bae, I am lying here for a little while." I realized that forgetting to take the trash out every weekend was bothering Laquita, so I took it upon myself to do what was right.

When I came back in, she was already in the kitchen cooking breakfast. "I thought you were going to stay in bed a little while?" "I was, but I realize my husband is up and he likes to eat." "You know me, honey, and I love you." I love you, too." "Look, next month I would like to have a card game here at the house and we'll invite all of our friends, what do you say?" "That sounds good to me, will we be playing your favorite game?" "Of course, you know I love playing spades, you do remember how to play, don't you?" "Yes, just like you taught me, why, will you and I be on teams?" "Yes, you are my partner for life." "I love that, okay, I will let the girls know, this should be fun," Laquita said with a smile on her face. "Bae, I would like to ask you a serious question." "What's that?" "I want us to start going to church, you know I am here with you for a lifetime, but I want both of us to go to heaven, we should work on our spiritual growth." "We are working on our spiritual growth; don't you pray every day?" "Yes, I do, but it takes more than you and I just praying, we need to start going to church." "Going to church, for what? I don't trust those Pastors." "What do the Pastors have to do with our believing in the Lord and wanting to be saved so our souls can go to heaven?"

"Pastors these days are all about making money; they have turned the church into a business." "I understand that, but you shouldn't let that keep you from going to heaven." "It won't, I don't need a Pastor to get me to heaven, all I need is a relationship with God." "That's true, but the Bible does say we need to attend church so we can worship God with other believers and be taught his word for our spiritual growth." "I am sure it does, but I just can't be around fakes." "Stop saying that, will you just think about it?" "I have already thought about it, and I just don't feel right about going to a church where the Pastors have private jets. What does a Pastor need with a private jet anyway?" "That's his business, that's not what you're going to church for, Bae."

"All these people do is take poor people's money." "Stop thinking like that, you can't believe that all churches do is take our money, the Bible says we should pay our tithes anyway." "What if I don't have any money? How am I going to tithe then?" "That's a crazy question because you have the money." I know I do, but I don't want to contribute to the Pastor driving a Bentley car, I mean, back in the days they had Cadillacs, I can deal with that, but now, they are in Maseratis and Bentleys, these cars are hundred-thousand-dollar cars." "That may be true, but I would like to be saved with my husband, I don't care what the Pastor drives." She said with a sad look on her face.

"Stop looking like that, you know what that does to me." "Looking like what, I just don't want us to go to hell." "I don't think God will let us go to hell if we live righteously as he told us." "Brent, what are you scared of?" "What am I scared of? I am not scared of anything. I've been to church lots of times, it's the people in the churches that I don't trust."

"If you can go play spades, then you can go to church." "Now, what do spades have to do with this?" "Everything, because you would rather go play spades with your sinning friends than go to church and learn the word." "That's not true, that's not a good comparison, but look, let me think about it, I can see how much it means to you." "It means a lot, we have been through so much, and it's time to give God his praise for keeping us together and keeping our marriage strong." "I pray to God all the time, I know he's been there for us, and he deserves it, his just do, but baby, these Pastors are flying in private jets." "Brent, it's not about him, let God handle those Pastors, it's not up to you." "He has a Bentley; they live in a mansion." "Brent, please, just think about it." "I am thinking about it, I will tell you this, let's find a poor black church, I mean let's find one that's so far back in the woods that no one can see it, and the floors still have shrubs growing in the corners of the church, ha, ha," I said in laughter. "Ha, ha, are you crazy, come on Bae, I am serious." "Hell, I am serious, ha, ha, I will think about it, okay, honey?" "I guess, just remember, I don't want to go to hell, I am going to start going back to church, and I don't want to be alone, I want to be with my husband." "I promise, I will think about it." "I am going to church next Sunday; I hope I am not going alone." "Next week, for real, that's not giving me enough time to think." "I am going to pray to God that he will change your heart, here, heat your breakfast, it has gotten cold." She said as she walked upstairs.

As much as I didn't want to go to church, I knew it would make my wife happy. I couldn't help but notice how these Pastors are living these days. They are becoming millionaires right under our noses. Although I had my opinion, I didn't want my soul to go to hell, and I tried to keep my wife and God happy. I sat and thought about it for hours, and I knew what I had to do. But first, I prayed about it.

The following Sunday came around, and I could see Laquita getting dressed for church. She didn't say a word to me. I jumped into the shower, got out, and dried off. "Why are you staring at me?" I asked. "No reason, what are you doing?" "I am getting dressed, why?" "Dressed for what, Steven's house?" "No, I am getting ready so I can

TWO HEARTS, TWO SOULS, ONE LIFE

attend church with my beautiful wife." "Ha, ha, are you serious?" She asked with a great big smile on her face. "Yes, I am going to church, for real." "Ahh, Bae, thank you so much." "I know how much it means to you, so I decided to make that step." "Don't do it for me, do it for yourself and God. We have a lot to be grateful for, Brent." "I know we do, and I will try not to look at the Pastor's Bentley." "Ha, ha, we are going to a poor black church, I think the Pastor drives a Lexus truck, he and his wife have one." "Ha, ha, I tell you, but I have to remember that's not what I am going for." "Yes, you do, God loves you, and that's why he brought me into your life." "So, you're here to save my soul?" "I am here as your helper and whatever you need, I am your ride-or-die chick, like the kids say these days," Laquita said with passion. "I love you, and thank you for the pep talk about going to church, now let's get dressed and go get spiritually fed. "I agree, let's hurry, so we can find a place to park," Laquita said.

We finished getting dressed and headed to church. We got a good parking spot, and we walked into the house of the Lord. After hearing a good word, it felt so good. Laquita turned to me and smiled as she grabbed my hand.

The Pastor's word was so powerful, and I was surprised. I felt everything he was saying. It felt like every word was meant for me to hear. By the time church was over, I was well-fed with the gospel. "Good afternoon, I hope you folks enjoyed the sermon, and I hope you will come again." Pastor Wilson said. "I will, I mean my wife and I, will be back, thank you, Pastor," I said. Laquita grabbed my hand, and she held it tight. As we walked out of the church, she whispered, "I love you, Bae, thank you for coming to church with me." "I love you, too. This was worth it." "God is working on you." "I know he is, but it will take time." "That's all God can ask for, trust in him, and you will make it to the Pearly Gates." "I do believe we will give God all the glory," I said. "Amen, Amen," Laquita noted, and we got into our car and headed home.

"I felt full of the spirit. I could feel something inside of me; it felt like butterflies, but deep down, I knew it was my spiritual growth growing within me.

That night I prayed to God for my life, for giving me such a beautiful and caring wife. I asked him to create miracles in my life, and I know that he could because he had already sent me the most beautiful thing in the world, my wife, Dr. Laquita Spade.

SPADE

18

PLAYING SPADES OVER OUR HOUSE

I woke up early Saturday morning once again. "Good morning, Bae, it's time to get up and get things ready for the spades party." "Yes, I know, but first let me get up and take this trash out, and then I will go into the garage and bring in three folded-up tables," I said. "You go ahead, baby. Oh, I took your clothes to the cleaners, and I got them out yesterday." "Thank you, honey, now let me get up," I said. "Bae, hand me my phone, it's ringing." "Okay, I am going now," I said. "Hello, hello, who is this?" "Tracy, hey girl, did you get my message the other day?" Tracy and I talked for a while, and then I got up to help Brent get things together.

"Who was that on the phone?" I asked. "That was Tasha's cousin, Tracy. I've been helping her out." "Helping her out how?" "I've been giving her some good advice; it seems as if she's taking it." "That's good, see that's why I love you; you're always helping everybody."

"It's in my blood, I love to help people, I just hope they are grateful when it's all said and done." "Will Tracy be coming to the spades party?" "No, she hasn't come that far yet." "Come that far, what?" "Ha, ha, it's nothing, she's healing right now, but Tasha is coming." "Okay, whatever that means," Brent said as we continued getting the house together for the spade's party.

I started cooking all the food. And, getting all the platters out that I bought early in the week. I pulled out five packs of cards and set them down on the kitchen table. Brent assembled all the tables, and we set them up. It took us hours to get the house just right.

All our friends started showing up at about 6 pm. "Hey Tasha, Portia, Sabrina, Linda," I said. "Hey, girl," Sabrina said. "Here comes Kemberley and her husband Michael, they were behind us," Tasha said. "Tasha, where is Jordan?" I asked. "He's coming, he said he will be here later," Tasha said. "Oh, your husband is in town?" Portia said. "Listen, don't start, we won't do this tonight, we will be kind to one another, and we will have fun, do I make myself clear?" I said.

"Laquita, tell your friends to come in," Brent said. The girls came in, and Michael and Kemberly followed shortly after. "Laquita, my husband Jimmy is on the way," Sabrina said. "I can't stand her husband," Portia said as she whispered to me. I shook my head because this woman doesn't know how to stop.

Shortly after, the doorbell rang, and all my friends were at the door. "Hey, Steven, Stanley, Carlos, y'all come on in," I said. "Hey Brent, are y'all ready to get spanked in spades?" Stanley asked. "Did someone say spanked?" Portia said, and everybody started laughing. "Leave it up to her to break the ice," Sabrina said. "I want everybody to introduce themselves as I finish getting things ready, honey, we need a few pads of paper and some pens, and then we will pick teams," I said. "Okay, Bae, I will go get them from the pantry," Laquita said.

"Steven, is your friend coming?" I asked. "No, she has to work tonight," Steven said as he walked towards me. "Yeah, she has to work all right, probably on another man," Stanley whispered to me. "Stop it, man, this evening is all about friends and family, I didn't want to hear any ragging in each other, we are around ladies, so we are going to show them that we are gentlemen," I said, and the fellas listened. "Hey, you guys, the food is ready if you want to eat. We have hors d'oeuvres and drinks," Laquita said.

"I am ready to play cards." Portia and Linda said. "My husband and I want to play," Kemberley said. "Can we get some cards over here? I am ready," Michael said. "We are going to kick some butt, tell them, honey." Kemberley said, "Y'all ready, huh?" Carlos said with a smirk on his face. "I don't care who's my partner, we're still going to win," Stanley said. "I am with you," Portia said. "Well, we will see, won't we?" Laquita said.

TWO HEARTS, TWO SOULS, ONE LIFE

"Brent, are we still going to be partners?" Steven asked. "Man, I am sorry, my wife and I are going to be partners, you better call your friend at work, ha, ha," I said sarcastically. "Now, that's cold, okay, okay, and when I do get a partner, we are coming for you and Laquita," Steven said. "Bring it on, Steven," Laquita said. "So, listen, we have three tables here, so everybody should get a chance to play, y'all pick your teams, all I know is my wife and I are on this table right here, so who's playing us?" I asked. "We want you guys first," Stanley said as he put his hand out to Portia. "That's right, we want to beat you guys on this table," Portia said as she smiled and blushed at the same time.

"Is that child blushing?" Tasha whispered to me. "Hush, girl," I said. "Oh, my God," Tasha said in a low tone. "Okay, guys, here go the pads and the pens, y'all can start playing at the other tables, and the final winner can come to this table because my wife and I ain't getting off this table, ain't that right, honey?" "You know it, Bae, ha, ha," Laquita said, and everybody started laughing.

As Laquita and I started kicking ass on the tables, a few more people showed up. We were so eager to beat everybody's ass on the table. Laquita and I beat Portia and Stanley pretty quickly. They tried to bogart and get to the other table, but no one was having it. The next couple to step up was Kemberley and Michael. They both like to talk a lot of shit on the table. So, Laquita and I matched their intensity, and we brought the pain. Kemberley and Michael nearly beat us, but my wife and I had some good chemistry; we knew how to call those cards. Every time I had a bad hand, she had a good hand, and vice versa. We kept getting all the good cards. "Y'all must be cheating, this is y'all's house and y'all's cards. "Portia said. "Are they cheating, Portia?" Linda asked as she was walking from table to table to see who her partner was going to be. "Yeah, they have to be cheating," Portia said. "Nobody is cheating, but we are winning," Laquita said. "Hey, can Linda and I play next? Your name is Linda, right?" Steven said. "Yes, it is, Steven, is it, right? Come on, let's play, Linda said with a smile on her face. "Linda, are you sure you and Steven want this?" I asked. "Bring it, we are ready," Linda said. "I see you're just like Steven, full of wishes," I said. "Man, come on and shuffle these cards," Steven said as he and Linda sat down.

After several rounds of spades against Linda and Steven, Laquita yelled, "Yes, they are set, baby, they are set." She puts one card in the air and slams it down, and it's a high joker. "Ha, ha, they set, they set, let me add this up." "Y'all are lucky or cheating over here," Steven said. "I know, right?" Linda said with a giggle. "No way, yall butts are set," Laquita said once more. "We got them, the points are 355 to 325, we win, we are the champs," I said, and my wife and I gave each other a high-five.

"Whatever. Whatever, everyone yelled. We both laughed. By the time, the night was over, Laquita and I had defeated every team. "That's right, the house rules," Laquita said loudly.

TWO HEARTS, TWO SOULS, ONE LIFE

When it was all said and done, no couple could take us off the table, so one by one, they made-to-go plates, and they left. The last ones to go were Stanley, Portia, Steven, and Linda. They were chatting and getting acquainted. Laquita and I started cleaning up some of the mess. When we turned around, Linda and Steven were walking out the door together, and so were Stanley and Portia. "Bye, guys, come back again and get your butts whooped," Laquita yelled. "Y'all won't be so lucky the next time," They yelled as they kept engaging with one another out of the door.

"That was fun, I enjoyed myself," Laquita said. "So, did I. We have to do that more often," I said. "I agree, can we just clean up the rest of this mess tomorrow?" Laquita said in exhaustion. "That's a good idea, I am going to take a shower and lie down," I said, and we headed upstairs.

I walked into the shower first, and I pressed my head against the wall as the hot water ran down my naked body. I put my hands over my face, and I started breathing in and out very slowly. Suddenly, I felt soft hands touch my flesh, and I turned. Laquita meshed her naked body to my back, and we both just let the hot water flow down our bodies. We stayed in that position for minutes. It felt so good to know she has my back, and I have hers. Together we mesh as one, and I love her dearly for being my helpmate.

My position is simple: I am her lover, best friend, confidant, and protector; I am her husband. Her place is my helpmate, my lover, my best friend, and sometimes, ha, ha, my boss; she is whatever she wants to be in our marriage because my love for her runs that deep. Her place is first. I hope you all get it!

The next morning, Laquita and I woke up and decided to go for a run. Soon as we opened the door, that damn black Impala was parked down the street again. We both looked at each other and shrugged our shoulders, then started jogging down the street. "I love you." I said, "I love you, too." She said. "I hope they find who they are looking for soon," I said. "I hope they do too," Laquita noted, and we just continued our jog together.

The End

TWO **HEARTS**, TWO **SOULS**, ONE **LIFE**

CHARLES LEE ROBINSON JR.

Written by

Charles Lee Robinson Jr.

TWO HEARTS, TWO SOULS, ONE LIFE

These days relationships and marriages don't aren't honored as they once were. People are so quick to judge and they are very impatient. I hear it all the time, "There's no more honesty or consistency." Most of the time the problem is both individual's problem, not just one person's. As you can see men and women have separate roles but sometimes, both roles are the same if the two individuals are okay with letting the other take charge or lead sometimes. You have to be willing to make this an "Us" thing and not just an "I" thing.

There are no perfect relationships, there are only imperfect people who put the effort into that relationship/marriage to work. A woman's place isn't a bad thing unless you're thinking negatively, and a man's position isn't a bad thing unless that individual tries to take control disrespectfully. Love is a two-way street, and failure is one way. Love who you're with as they love you and your roles will become natural, and not suggested.

Author Charles Lee Robinson Jr.

CHARLES LEE ROBINSON JR.

Made in United States
Orlando, FL
15 August 2025